ASYLUM

GARY ROME

This is a work of fiction. Names, characters, places, and incidents either are the product of the author's imagination or are used fictitiously. Any resemblance to actual persons, living or dead, events, or locales is entirely coincidental. Discretion is advised as this book contains content which may not be suitable for young readers.

Book Editing and Layout Design by Jay T. Hatman
Editor Webpage: www.hatman.us
Cover Image © 2016 by Oleg Magni
Image URL: www.pexels.com/photo/abstract-art-black-background-blur-1040499

United States Library of Congress Control Number
2020915384

First editions originally self-published through Barnes & Noble, Inc. and Amazon.com, Inc. in 2020

ISBN Paperback
978-1-64999-634-3
979-8-69335-661-0 (Amazon)
ISBN Hardcover
978-1-64999-635-0

Copies of this book are printed in the United States of America unless noted otherwise *to my best friends and brothers, Dann and Joshua, who pushed me to make my book longer.*

to Duane, for helping immensely to put together the first draft.

to my boss Brandon, for putting up with my craziness.

to Colin, my partner in crime with outside marketing.

last, and certainly never least, to my beautiful daughter Raven. You light up my world.

Asylum. asy·lum | \ ə- sī-ləm *[noun]*

An asylum is a prison, a state of isolation of the mind and the body. It is where one goes to think; to be incarcerated. An asylum is a place to forget and to be forgotten. It is a haven as well as a nightmare, both physical and mental.

CHAPTER 1

"Oh, God, where... where am I?! What happened to me? I can hardly remember anything after getting off the phone with Liz about Amber's birthday dinner." James sat up in the middle of the floor in a nearly dark, unknown room, exclaiming his confusion. He placed his hand upon his forehead. "Ahh, my head. It feels fuzzy. It's so dark in here." James looked around the room, confused. "I can barely make anything out in this room." His eyesight was still a bit blurry from waking up, trying to focus his sight on anything he could in the room. *The ground feels hard and cold like it could be made of stone or maybe even tile,* James thought as he passed his hands along the hard, rough surface.

He then noticed a small beam of light on the ground. James looked up and saw a dim, yellowish light illuminating outside of what looked to be a tiny window within the upper-middle of the door. There was just enough light coming in for James to make out the dark and rusted steel door below. His eyes grew wide with fear as he wondered if he had just awoken in some kind of prison cell. James noticed the small light outside the room swaying back and forth ever so slightly as he heard what sounded like the rattling of rusted chains.

James tried to stand up to see what might be causing the light to swing as well as determine the source of the sound. As soon as he attempted to get to his feet, however, he fell hard to the ground. "Fuck!" he screamed in pain. "I can hardly put any pressure on my right leg." James grabbed his leg and brought it up to his chest, bellowing as a sharp, searing pain began to shoot down his leg.

"It seems my right leg is useless. I can`t even see what the fuck is wrong with it because of the lack of light in here," he snarled to himself angrily. The room was eerily quiet; even the most minute noise sounded as if a freight train were racing through the halls at full speed.

James soon began to hear noises all around him in the darkness. The clamor grew ever louder with each passing second. There was the rushing sound of thousands of tiny, needle-like feet scraping on the dark stone walls. There appeared to be hundreds of roaches, some tiny, some large, scurrying along the walls, he thought, as he cradled his leg. James also heard the twitching sound of rats as they edged along the bottom wall. "The room, it feels cold," James sighed as he crawled his way towards the nearest wall. Leaning his back up against it, he soon discovered that every inch of its' surface felt very damp and sticky. It was as if the room itself had been sweating.

James stretched his arm out to inspect the wall. As he passed his hand up and down along its' rough surface, a thousand different questions began to race through his head. "Who put me here? What day is it... and why is my head throbbing so badly?"

The pain was so unbearable that James could hardly think. He felt as if he would faint at any second now. He passed his right hand down the back of his head, feeling a warm, thick liquid matting his hair.

Just then, an anonymous voice called forth from seemingly nowhere. "Go to the window!"

"Who are you?!" James yelled back, feeling very confused. "Are you trapped in here like me?!"

He waited several minutes for a response but was greeted with nothing but eerie silence. The only thing he could hear was his voice echoing inside the emptiness of his cell. James got up and tried to walk to the window, though as soon as he pushed his body weight off of the wall he fell right back to the floor again. “Fuck! God damn it!” he roared at the walls in pain.

James looked up at the small window and began to crawl towards it. He proceeded to eke himself across the floor towards the opposite side of the room, heading to what appeared to be a door. The ground was mucked in an ever-increasing layer of filth as he made his way toward the opening, staining his white, button-down shirt and navy blue dress pants in the process. “I made it,” James sighed in a brief bout of happiness. His lungs were toiling quite heavily now. As he drew in his labored breaths, James noticed a rotten smell permeating the air. “Oh, God, what is that?” he exclaimed, covering his mouth with his left hand as he propped himself up along the wall nearest the door. He decided to rest for a while to try and steady his breathing and gather his thoughts.

Several minutes passed. After what seemed to be an eternity, James pulled himself up to the small window with the assistance of the bronze door handle. “What the hell is this? The window has iron bars on it! What kind of place is this?” James shouted at himself in great frustration. He wrapped his hands around the cold steel bars and tugged on them with all his might.

“Okay, now what?!” he exclaimed at the walls. The mysterious voice from earlier responded with maniacal laughter.

“Check your hand,” it commanded.

Puzzled, James shouted back, “My hand?”

"Yes," the voice responded. "Place your hand between the bars; use the one you used to rub the back of your head with." Still confused a bit, James shoved his right hand through the bars and into the night glow.

James was horrified to see that his hand was covered in his blood. "What the...? How did he know that there was blood on my hand?" James asked himself in a whispered tone. He was still in disbelief. James tried over and over to ask the mysterious voice how he knew that his hand had blood on it, but his inquiry fell on deaf ears. Taken back by what had just occurred, James slumped his way back upon the filthy floor. He slowly crept his way towards the door. As he laid there with his back upon its' surface, he began to think of his wife and daughter and how he may never see them again. That fear, the realization that he might die in this place, slowly started to sink in. "I have to get out of this place," James told himself. As he slowly pulled himself up to his feet, he placed his left hand on the handle of the doorknob and tried to open it. Despite everything, nothing happened. The handle refused to budge.

"Locked... fuck!" James shouted in anger. He passed his hand along the bottom of the door's handle while leaning on its' surface for balance, trying to feel for a keyhole. *If there is one then I could try and force the door open*, he thought to himself, trying to exhibit a veneer of courage within his inner voice. Suddenly, James' right leg gave out and he collapsed back onto the floor. He once again found himself on the dirty, sludge caked ground crawling in the dark like a blind, helpless baby. He passed his hands around on the stone surface from right to left, trying to find anything with which he could use to pry open the cell door.

"Oh, God, the smell in this room is unbearable." James cried as he tried to hold back his vomit. The sheer rottenness of the odor was making it hard for him to do so. His eyes started to sting as tears blurred his vision. James began to cough as the foul stench burned his nose, the faint taste of rotten eggs and spoiled milk cresting his tongue and lingering within the back of his throat. James continued to pass his hand along the floor through what can only be described as vile, rotten filth. Parts of his clothes began to soak with whatever nastiness had coated the ground. The slush-like substance seemed only center itself near the door; nothing appeared to cover the space from where James first awoke. Eventually, his right hand found itself dipped into a small puddle. "Fuck, I really hope that is not piss I just put my hand in," he exclaimed, mortified. Despite the implications, James continued along with his search. After what seemed like forever, his hand finally came across something small but sharp. The object felt as if it might be part of an ice pick. *But why would this be in here? Who would leave a broken ice pick in this room and why?* James wondered. *Huh. Maybe the last person in here was trying to get out of this place as well.* He picked up the ice pick and made his way back towards the door.

As he continued along with his newfound mission, he pulled himself up to the window, glancing out of the opening one last time to see if anyone might be out there. No; it was just a creepy, empty hallway staring back at him. He placed the sharp point of the ice pick into the keyhole and began trying to force the lock open. With a few good hits of the palm of his left hand, the door was now unimpeded.

James slowly opened the rusted metal door. A collection of dust previously resting upon the top of the wooden frame began to fall. The powder fell like thick, heavy, grayish snow. The loud shrieking sound of rusted hinges scraping metal echoed like thunder throughout the hallway. James silently wondered what had happened to the person that was in this room before him.

The door now laid fully opened. To his amazement, the hallway was a bit longer than it had first appeared through the window. It was poorly lit and looked to be completely caked in filth. Nobody seems to have bothered cleaning up the place in quite some time. James could hear roaches running along the walls, but he could hardly see them in the gloom. They appeared as only large black spots zipping along the wall. Some rats were running along the baseboards of the floor within the hallway. James noticed a single rusted pendant light fixture in the hallway hanging from the ceiling.

The chain slowly swayed back and forth. The lights protruding from the fixtures were very dim. James was barely able to make out crumbling chunks of popcorn ceiling finish which were peeling and hanging down towards the floor. There was ripped, yellow-stained wallpaper covering the walls of the corridor. To his best guess, the main power was dead and only the emergency lighting circuit was functioning. It explained why James could barely see his shadow on the floor, let alone the outlines of any other doors in the hallway. James used the surface of the walls to assist him in navigating the dark corridor. The ground was covered in the white tile which would perhaps have a pearly finish if kept clean. Some of the stones were chipped and cracked. Several dark and dried stains were smeared upon the ground's surface, adding to the blemish of filth.

"Are you there?" James shouted. Only the sound of the mystery voice laughing echoed back towards him. "Who the fuck are you?!" he shouted again, red with anger down the poorly lit hallway.

A brief silence beckoned back towards James. Then, softly, as if remanding a child, the voice finally answered back. "We will meet in due time, friend... in due time."

James started to feel dizzy again thanks to the loss of blood from his head wound. His skull continued to throb in pain. *I need to make my way to the right side of the hallway*, he told himself. The wound was throbbing with even more anguish now. Feeling faint, James dropped to one knee. He shook his head clear, picked himself back up, and tried to make his way to the opposite side of the hallway before his leg once again buckled. He fell towards the floor. Crawling along the ground after a minute he reached his intended wall. He used its' surface to lift himself once again. Once on his feet again, James noted that the hallway had a very eerie feel to it. *The loss of blood and the overbearing pain must be taking effect*, thought James as he began to notice what he thought could be movement in the dark.

Wow, my mind must be playing tricks on me. I thought I had just seen someone move. Just a few feet from me. I must be hungry. I can't even remember when the last time I ate was nor what I even ate, James thought as he continued to make his way down the hallway. He found what looked to be an old, somewhat long, raggedy broom handle. The base of the broom was missing. "Great!" James shouted as he picked up the wooden handle. The broom handle was very thick. James surmised that he could use this handle as a makeshift crutch. He tried placing the wooden stick under his right armpit. It was when he laid his weight upon the stick that James discovered it was shorter than he had first thought. "Well, guess I'll have to use it as a cane for now instead of a crutch," James said. The stick barely made it passed his waist. He placed his right hand over the top of the wooden stick. It was time to get out of this place.

As he began to walk, James could hear the sound of a faint giggle. "Hello? is there anyone there?" James asked the darkness, looking down the expanse of the empty hallway. The lights began to flicker wildly as if even the auxiliary power was going to die out. Soon all the lamps began to sway rapidly from side to side.
A chilling breeze shot past James. As he kept shouting the same question the giggling kept getting louder and louder. As sudden as the lights began swaying, they came to a complete stop. To James' relief, the strange giggling also ceased.

James felt as if he were being watched. The hair on his arms as well as his neck started to rise as goosebumps began to surface on his arms. James waited to see if the giggling would return, but, nothing; no laughter nor any other sound could be heard within the hallway. The only sound James could make out was the loudness of his heart beating.

After a moment, James decided to press onward down the corridor. The unpleasant aroma of mold along with a musk-like smell filled the hallway. James soon came to find a crossway in the middle of the long stretch. The center of this crossway was a good size, about twenty feet across from each corner of the four passageways connecting to it. Leaning up against one of the edges, James gazed into the three paths he had yet to venture down. The cold, dry air started to slowly creep upon James again as he inspected each of the passages. He needed to figure out which one might lead him out of this hellish place. He looked down the left passageway as much as he could, but the hallway was completely blacked out; no light seemed to emanate from its' reaches. James thought that he would be helpless if he were to venture down that path. He looked down the remaining two corridors; the right hallway had the same poor visibility as the one that he'd previously emerged from.

James decided to walk down the hallway to the right as the corridor straight ahead laid too far away from where he perched. Carefully, James took his hand from the wall which was helping him to stand. His right leg began to wobble as he used the wooden handle of his "cane" to help him walk.
Slowly, he inched his way towards the opposite wall of this new passage. "Damn it, I feel like a baby who's just learning how to crawl for the first time," James yelled out in frustration. As he took a few more steps, the cane gave out and he fell swiftly onto the ground. "Fuck! God damn it!" he shouted as intense pain coursed through his body.

The aches attacking his body were so horrendous that tears were being drawn upon James' eyes. He slowly began to drag himself along the floor toward his intended wall. After what seemed like hours, he finally made his way out of the crossway and into the corridor on the right. James slumped onto the floor and rested himself for a few minutes, finally finding the wall and using its' surface to pull himself up. *I can't keep relying on these walls to get myself around. I have to find something I can use to help stabilize this cane so that I can walk,* James surmised. As he made his way down the new path he began to spot the outlines of several doors.

Before I leave this place I must find out who put me here and why. James decided to make his way towards the first door.

Once he reached the entryway, James noticed there was a number etched into it. 621. James tried to open the door but it was locked. Damn! James thought to himself. *I have nothing to open the door with. Why did I leave the ice pick back inside the cell door where I was trapped in?* The door before him featured a small glass window in the center that was nearly blacked out from an unknown stain.

Once he decided he couldn't open this door, James then made it to the second one. This door was similar to the first one; it was a locked door but the stained window had a little bit more visibility to it. He pressed his face up against the window to see if he could spy anything in the room. The room had a little bit of light emitting from it. James could only make out the silhouette of a few boxes. *I wonder what's inside of those containers?* James asked himself before moving away from the window. He continued along the corridor, trying each door as he came upon them. After a few unsuccessful tries, James finally made it to a door the was slightly opened. He looked at the etching on the door.

Dr. Coffin Office. Room 615.

"Who the hell is Dr. Coffin?" James asked himself as he slid open the door.

The dim light from the hallway only illuminated the room slightly. It was just bright enough that James could make out what looked to be an old wooden desk with some paperwork on top of it. "Well, If I am gonna find out anything about what this place is and who put me in here, then I have to get inside this room to see if there are any clues to help me," James said out loud as he entered the room.

James flipped a nearby switch but the fixtures inside the room did not turn on. The hallway lamps illuminated the room like a child's dim night light. It was hardly enough light for James to use to look around. Despite this limitation, James made his way towards the desk in the center. Papers laid spread out in a messy pile on top of the wooden desk along with some folders. The tan files were caked in the dust; the ink upon the top pages had been faded with time. One folder, in particular, caught James' eye.

This folder was labeled in bold print, “Dr. Coffin.” He grabbed the entire folder and made his way back into the doorway. James sat on the floor, leaned himself on the entry frame, and began to read the papers in the folder.

CHAPTER 2

Date 10/23/1981 *St. Mary's Hospital*
Case # 094511 *for the Insane*

Hello, my name is Dr. Jason Coffin. Today I am going to see if case number 094511 can finish my little experiment. He is the 34th test subject that will try this; the others all failed to finish due to their insane mental breakdowns. They kept screaming on and on about a demon or something of that nature lurking in the shadows. I can barely understand what they are saying, but I do know from what I understand that they have all said the same thing. They have told my staff numerous times that they felt like something was always watching them from inside the darkness. Some even claimed to have heard laughter when no one was around. Their mental state was too far gone. So, to fix this small nuisance, I killed them.

I have selected a new subject by giving him a few tests. His name is of little importance. After he passed these tests, I had the night cook to prepare a special stew for him. This stew contains large trace amounts of the skin, brain matter, fats, and meats as well as small trace amounts of urine, blood, and ground-up bones from the previous test subjects mixed in with a heavy sleep sedative. After several minutes of holding down the test subject and forcing the food down his throat, he had soon passed out. I ordered the night guards to then go into his cell and strip him out of those filthy garments he was wearing and put new clothes on him. The shirt and pants that he now wears have serval patches sewn into them. Those patches are made from some of the skin of the dead test subjects who failed. The rest of their skins have been woven together to make the subject's bedsheets. I will now leave him in the cell, isolated from any human contact for thirteen weeks with no light. I will give him very little food and water. After his mind is nearly driven mad with insanity, I will let him out to see if he can escape my maze. If he succeeds in making it out, I'll take him to the altar and he will be the next one sacrificed in our ritual of blood.

"Oh, God, that's awful. This Dr. Coffin is fucking sick," James said out loud as he finished reading the last page. "This doctor would use those poor, mentally handicapped people as his play-things? Leaving them trapped in his twisted, sick maze of horror? God, those poor souls." James couldn't help but summon images of what he was reading to flood his mind. He couldn't hold the sick feeling he had in anymore, quickly hunching over to throw up on the floor.

"Oh, man, that was disgusting," James said as he wiped away the remnants of yellow-green bile from his mouth with the back of his right hand. "Those images will be forever burned into my mind. I need to get out of this place and find out just who the fuck put me in here. Liz, Amber... Daddy will be home soon, I promise." James exited the room and continued to make his way down the long hallway. As he advanced his way further down the corridor, James noticed the air had suddenly changed. The atmosphere was now drier and heavier than it had been previously.

A sense of foreboding washed over James like vertigo. Out of instinct, he looked behind him, only to find that all the lights down the hallway were going dark. One by one, as if there was someone or something invisible that James couldn't see, was unscrewing each of the bulbs. James watched, frozen with fear, as a thick, dark swirling cloud of mist slowly engulfed the hallway. He soon realized that he had to get somewhere safe. James quickly turned around and started to walk as fast as he could; his visibility was dampening as the lights in front of him began to disappear. James was now stuck in the middle of the hallway, the darkness now closing in on him from both sides.

He simply stood there, feeling trapped; James could feel his heart pounding rapidly in his chest as if it were about to break out. *Thump... thump... thump... thump...* the sound of his heart echoed loudly through the corridor.

As the dark mist crept ever closer towards James, he could hear an evil, low tone of laugher coming from deep within the black void. The chilling presence of the racket made James petrified with fear. At first, the laughter sounded as if it were coming from right in front of him; then, James imagined that it was emerging from behind him. Before long, he realized that the unholy chuckling was emanating from all around him. With every second, the darkness grew closer and closer towards James; the cackling grew louder and more demonic. In the blink of an eye, James was soon surrounded by a thick, dark mist. The abysmal emptiness did not fully engulf James; it stopped just a foot shy from him.

James looked up and observed that he stood under the only light in the hallway which was still illuminated. He could feel an incredibly evil presence engulfing the entirety of the mist. As he stood frozen in place, sweat began to bead upon his forehead. The fear of not knowing what laid within the dark gale made his heart race.

"This is it," James mouthed to himself in a barely audible whisper. "I will never see my wife and daughter again." He closed his eyes and tears began to stream down his face. He could feel the intense pressure of a horrid being standing close behind him. Suddenly, James felt the heaviness of what seemed to be a hand pressing down ever so lightly on his left shoulder. The digits that gripped James' shoulder did not feel like a normal human hand. The fingers felt as if they were long, thin, and boney.

The being's hair was long, gray, and mossy; some of its' strands were longer than others, each whisker separated inches due to a severe case of androgenic alopecia. The nails curved inward, digging into James' chest like the sharp talons of a bird of prey. Right before James blacked out from the sheer weight of terror, he felt the thing lean in close to his ear. James started to pray in a hushed tone. "Our father, who art in heaven, hallowed be thy name." As James continued to beg his words of solace, he could feel the hot, stinking breath coming from the apparition's mouth as it whispered with sinister pleasure into James' ear: "Run, little rabbit, run." A white flash of light glazed over James. Everything turned to black as he collapsed on to the floor in pure fright.

...

"James, James, hey James," a voice echoed faintly in the distance. "Hey, welcome back buddy. You feeling okay, man?" James opened his eyes to look at the tall fair-skinned man with brown eyes and short dark hair. It was Josh, James' friend, and coworker. "Yeah, long night," James replied, noting that his voice was coming through loud and clear. James looked down, noted he was standing in front of a sink, and splashed some water on his face.

"So, James, how is it going with your case?"

"Well, you know what they say, Josh... it's, umm, it's going. I feel like I am having some trouble convincing the jury that my client is innocent." Josh, standing at the sink next to James, began washing his hands and James unconsciously followed suit. "Don't worry, James, you'll get them to come around and see your point on the matter. You always do," replied Josh, a slight smirk upon his face. Both men were wearing clean, crisp business suits; Josh with the tan, cream-colored

three-piece suit while James sported a dark blue suit. They left the men's room and headed for the nearby break room.
"Oh, hey, your little girl's birthday is coming up soon, right?" Josh asked.

"Yeah, Amber will be turning thirteen this Friday."

The pair entered the break room. The room was not fancy, small with pale white walls upon which hung a handful of inspirational posters. A few small, round wooden tables laid spread out. Each table featured about six dark plastic chairs. On the far wall of the room was a small, black 1200-watt microwave, a sink, and a stainless steel refrigerator. Next to the fridge were a few cabinet drawers that held small paper cups, napkins, and a host of other condiments.

"Man, thirteen already, she has grown up so fast," Josh said as he made his way to the refrigerator.

"Yeah, she is," James replied, reminiscing in his mind on the days when his daughter was small.

"Better watch out, man, soon the boys will be coming over," Josh followed up, the smirk from before once again gracing upon his face.

James smiled back. "Not going to happen."

"So, what are you and Liz doing for Amber's birthday?" asked Josh.

"Well, Liz and I are thinking about taking her out to eat Friday night after I get home from work."

"That sounds nice. Speaking of food, what did you bring for lunch today?" Josh asked James, changing the subject.

“The wife made me a cob salad with baked chicken breast. She said I need to start watching what I eat,” replied James in a somber tone.

“Oh, nice. I brought some leftovers from my house. It’s Chinese that picked up last night at the Red Dragon, y’ know, down on the corner of 8th and Long St.” That joking smile once again crept onto Josh’s face. “Hey, wanna trade?” James knew better than to reply; Josh’s food had already been popped into the microwave when he said this.

As they both sat down at one of the break room tables to eat, James' cell phone began to ring. He reached into his left pocket, took out his phone and answered it. “Oh, hi hun,” he told his wife. “Hi, babe,” the voice on the phone said back. “I just called to check up on you. How is work going?” asked Liz.

“It’s going okay; this case is tough. The defense is trying to play every strategy in the book that they can so my client doesn’t walk,” he tells her in between bites of food.

“Well you will win, I have faith. How’s the salad? Did I pack enough?”

“Yes dear, the salad is great and you packed more than enough for me.”

“Oh, good!” exclaimed Liz with a slight sigh of relief. “So, James, did you make the dinner reservations for this Friday?”

“Yes, dear, I did,” James tells her. He takes another bite of the salad. Josh is sitting on the opposite side of the table munching on a half-eaten eggroll. He watches James’ facial expression changed slightly. That trademark smirk graced Josh's face. “Thank God I don’t have kids yet, let alone a girl that’s about to turn thirteen,” he said out loud as he finished the eggroll.

“Seven p.m. at Perez's Italian Restaurant,” James said into the phone.

“Great. Amber will be thrilled that we’re going to her favorite place to eat. Oh, by the way… her birthday gift is ready for pickup up at the store. So, after work, can you swing by and pick it up?”

“Yes, dear, I’ll pick up Amber’s birthday gift when I get off of work,” he said, rolling his eyes. He wasn’t going to forget.

“James, please make sure that you get it wrapped, okay? I don’t want Amber to find out what we got her.”

“I will get it wrapped, don’t worry,” he told Liz, continuing to munch on his food as he did.

“James,” Liz said in her more demanding voice now. “Don’t forget.”

“Okay, okay, I won’t forget to pick it Amber’s present up and get it wrapped,” James assured Liz as he looked up at the clock hanging on the wall. “Hey, hun, my lunch break is almost up. I’ll call you when I am on my way home after I pick up Amber’s gift, okay?”

“Ok hun, I love you,” Liz said. “Love you too,” James said back to her before he hung up the phone.

“So, dinner and a gift, too,” Josh said as he got up from the table to throw away his trash.

“Yeah, Amber loves this Italian restaurant call Perez’s. Her favorite dish there is the four meat and cheese lasagna and the triple-double hot fudge lava cake,” James told Josh as he started to pack up his lunch. “Oh, that sound so much better than this fast-food Chinese crap I bought last night. What do you and Liz get there when y’all go?”

"Well, Liz always gets the stuffed mushrooms and I get the baked chicken breast with spaghetti," James told Josh.

Josh looked into the mirror that was near the door, fixing his tie with one hand. "So what did kind of gift did you and Liz buy her?" he asked James, eager to know.

"Well, me and Liz thought about it, and since Amber is turning thirteen this year and she has shown us how responsible and mature she is... we bought her a cell phone." James put his unfinished leftovers in the refrigerator.

"Oh, nice!" exclaimed Josh.

"Yeah, we will put her on our cell plan," James told him as they started heading to the door.

"Oh, wow, now your phone bill will be bigger than the NASA electric bill," Josh said jokingly as the pair walked out of the lunchroom.

"Don't remind me," James said with a fake grimace. The two colleagues were laughing as James turned off the light to the break room.

CHAPTER 3

As James walked out of the break room, a bright light suddenly engulfed his sight. James soon found himself back inside the same filthy cell that he had previously woken up inside before. "Did I just dream that? If felt real, as if I were reliving what I did before waking up in this place," he wearily told himself, trying to regain his composure. "The last thing I can remember was passing out in a hallway. Why am I back in this room? Who put me back in the room?" James's mind raced with more questions, but the odor of the room made it hard for him to think. *Oh, God, that smell. It smells worse than before,* James thought to himself once he noticed that the stench was now more pronounced than ever. He looked around the room and noted that something was different than when he had first awoken in the room earlier. Not with the room itself, but for him. He was different; his clothes were different. The clothes that James was wearing had been changed.

James found himself in old, grayish, ragged, stained clothes. "Who put this on me and where are my clothes at?" James asked himself, looking at what he was now wearing. There was a dark, dried stain on the front of his shirt. There were several different color patches scattered upon the shirt as well. James noticed on the upper-right hand side of this shirt above his right breast was the serial number *70891*. The number was almost all but faded. "What the fuck is this? I… I remember reading something about this but it's not very clear. It's as if someone had erased it from my mind," James muttered as he tugged on the shirt. It was then that he had noticed on his left wrist was a patient ID bracelet. As he looked at the bracelet he found that the ID bracelet had the same serial number as the shirt: *70891*. Along with the number was his full name and date of birth.

James looked around the cell again to see if anything else had changed. *No,* he thought, *the room still looks the same; dark, gross, crawling with rats and roaches.* James put on a pretend to smile as he tried to get to his feet but found that he couldn't find the strength to will himself back up. "Wait, where is my cane?" he asked himself, panicking as he frantically began searching the floor looking at it. "Did I lose it? No... no, it has to be here!"

Just then his eyes were drawn out into the hallway by a shining object. *My cane... why is it out in the hallway?* A bit puzzled, James crawled on the floor out into the hallway to grab the broken broomstick. He then used the wall as well as the wooden stick to help him get back to his feet. James stood up, still puzzled about what had happened. He ran his hand across the back of his head again. *No blood... my wound must have healed.* He looked back at the inside of the cell on more time. *Okay, now I have to find a way out of this place. I need to find out who put me in here. I bet I'll probably find the answers hidden somewhere in this God-forsaken place.*

He looked at an old rusted metal plaque above his cell door. Carved into the old rusted plaque was the number *666.*

After what seemed like forever and a day, James made it back to the spot where he passed out from overwhelming fear of what was dwelling inside the darkness. Faintly, he could hear the crying and scream of a mother, and her laughter echoing in his head. Then, the voice of the thing he encountered. *"Run, little rabbit, run."* James tilted his head down. That voice was still fresh in his head. "It felt like all my hopes, all my dreams, were gone," James said, the soft-spoken words trembling with each breath as they left his mouth. "Everyone that I have ever loved was suddenly turned into ash and there was nothing left but darkness, emptiness.

As it pulled me deeper and deeper into the dark void… I felt nothing but fear, agony, dread, misery, and, above all, loneliness. The despair of never seeing my family, of never watching my daughter grow up. Never taking her to dances or walking her down the aisle of her wedding day. The fear of never growing old with Liz, my love, my soulmate, my better half. Never hearing her voice or seeing her sweet smile or feeling her warm touch. I… I never want to feel that again." A few tears gently kissed the sides of his cheeks as they slowly raced down his face. James paused for a moment at the spot where he blacked out. With his head still lowered, James reminded himself what he is fighting for. He then shook his head to clear the doubts and pick back up on his mission. He needed to see his family again.

As he continued to walk through the hallways, James had his makeshift cane gripped tightly in his left hand while also using the walls as an extra source of stability. After some time, he came across a door that read office room *604. There might be some kind of clue inside the room here to help me figure out just who the fuck put me in this hell hole.* James grabbed the old rusted brass doorknob with his right hand and turned it. The door had not been used in quite some time. It seemed almost impossible to open due to the collection of dust built up between the wooden frame and the metal door. A loud, eerie shriek bellowed throughout the long corridor as James opened the door.

The hairs on James' arm stood upright as if someone just passed an electrically charged balloon across his arms. He was afraid someone, or something, might have heard the loud noise and would come rushing down the hall at any moment. James quickly made his way into the suite. *It looks just like the last room I was in,* he thought. This room had just as poor of lighting as the room he had originally found.

James was able to make out some old file cabinets judging by their shapes. As he dug through them, he kept finding nothing but overdue bills as well as a foreclosure notice.

"Huh. So, from the looks of these unopened letters, they didn't have enough money to keep this place running and that's why they had to shut it down," James said in a low tone as he tossed the paperwork back into the drawers.

James then came across a small brown envelope face down on the desk. He picked up the package and turned it over to see if there was any writing on its' front. The face of the envelope was naked. As James ripped open the package, a small movie reel dropped out. "Okay??" James exclaimed as he was a bit puzzled why a projector tape would be hidden in there in the first place. After examining the reel, he looked around for a projector but could not find one. A brief thought crossed James' mind that he couldn't remember ever seeing one since his days in college. James looked at the reel; there was something written on the side. Most of the ink had faded away with time but he could make out:

08/12/82. Play Me. ~Dr. Coffin

"I have to find a projector and see what is in this film. It might have some kind hint as to who put me here," James said to himself. He checked the desk one more time. In the bottom drawer was a small blade. It was rusty and dull. *I don't think this blade can even cut through paper now that it's all worn down. I'll leave it here, then.* James closed the drawer and left the room. He decided there was nothing more in there that could help him.

The moment James walked out of the room and into the hallway, he could feel his right leg growing weaker by the minute.

More questions were racing in his head. *Why did this happen to me? Who put me here? Will I ever get see my wife and daughter again?* An image of his girls blowing him a kiss before he left for work came rushing to the front of his mind.

His wife Liz and his daughter Amber are standing in the front doorway of their home, the bright morning sun beaming down on them. His wife is wearing a sexy blue dress that just seemed to hug her figure exactly right. The dress had a slick v-neck opening that shows off a nice pink diamond necklace draped over her plump bosom. It was a necklace that James had purchased her for her birthday. Amber was wearing a black t-shirt with big bold red letters that read KISS on it with ripped jeans. Suddenly, both of their garments turned to pure black. Their faces were wearing see-through black veils and they were looking down onto a grave crying. The sky is no longer sunny but is dark and full of rain.

"Is that what will happen to me?" whispered James. "Will the last time my wife and daughter ever see me be at my funeral? They are burying me. No," James said, whisper turning into an angry shout, "I can't let that happen." Now he was more determined than ever to see his family.

James made his way to the elevator. After some time, he found himself at the end of the hallway. He stopped in front of the reflective metal doors of an elevator. James was taken aback, but not all too surprised, to find that there were four large two-by-four wooden bars nailed across the elevator door. James stopped and thought to himself for a moment. *Boarded, huh? Well, I doubt this place has enough power to even make it move one foot. Even if this old piece of junk worked it would more than likely break, plunging me to my death quicker than the fall of Napster.*

James, proud of his own joke, briefly smirked before heading towards what appeared to be a nearby set of stairs. Entering the doorway, he began to make his descent.

Fuck, this might have been a bad idea, James thought to himself. Each step he took was more painful than the last. *The first thing I am going to do when I get out of this place is to go straight home and give my daughter a big hug. I'll tell her how much I love her. I'll order myself a nice, juicy double cheeseburger from Burger King, grab myself a bottle of vodka, and make love to my wife all night. Yep, that is what I'm going to do.* James was deeply determined that he will see his wife and daughter again very soon. He was trying to block out the pain from his mind. James' heaving was becoming heavier and heavier with each step he took. After what felt like a long and agonizing few minutes, James reached the door to the fifth floor. He paused for a moment before opening the door. "Finally made it," he said, wheezing out of breath, gasping for new air. "I... I made it to the... the door." He leaned himself on the wall, eyes fixed on the faded white door.

CHAPTER 4

James opened the entrance leading onto the fifth floor. “It looks the same as the hallway from upstairs,” he stared in amazement as his eyes scanned the long, creeping corridor. “I wonder if all the floors’ hallways in this hospital look the same.” The hallway had a very uneasy feel to it to James as he navigated the dark, foreboding passageways. “Liz must be very upset and worried about me for not coming home.” He tried to keep his mind on something other than the creepy place he was in. James then realized that he had been talking to himself out loud. He laughed. “I can’t believe I’ve been talking like this, as if someone else is here. I guess maybe it’s because hearing my voice is comforting. It’s better than hearing the dead silence… or maybe it’s because I’m terrified.”

He came across the entryway to a dark room. The door didn’t feature any numbers on it but it was lying wide open. James carefully made his way into the room. He tried searching the area the best he could but the lack of light still made it hard for him to see anything. “A dead end… this room is too dark. I don’t think that there is anything of use to me in here.” The air turned to an almost deathly chill, and the same foreboding feeling from earlier once again overtook James. He noticed the lights above him had been swaying as before, spotted just in time to see them suddenly stop moving. The bulbs were abruptly dying. Rats and roaches were rushing down the hallway, seemingly in a perfect single-file line, trying to get away from whatever malevolent presence was enveloping the passageway.

Scared, James turned his body slightly to the right to look down the path where he just came from. His eyes were now fixated on the window of the stairway door.

James stood in the middle of the hallway now, nervously watching as the lights on the other side of the door turned off. The stairwell was now pitch dark. James' eyes grew wide with fear as the hatch started to open. A thick, grayish, heavy mist started to slowly pour out of the now pitch-black stairwell like dry ice from a smoke machine. Just as it had before, the mist started to slowly engulf the hallway.

James quickly turned and began to dash as fast as he could down the hallway. "Fuck... if my right leg wasn't so badly damaged I could run faster," he said to himself in anger as he felt his heart starting to beat faster in his chest with every passing second. He followed the rats down the corridor to safety. "I can't let the darkness get me. I don't want to encounter that nasty entity again." It seemed that when James moved faster, the darkness pursued with even more quickness. He could feel the chilling cold presence of evil creeping upon him as he barged into the slightly open entryway of a nearby room. James then felt a shock go through his body as he fell onto the grungy floor.

He quickly turned around and slammed the door behind him. His heart was still racing in his chest with fear. James' breathing was still heavy as he pinned his back up against the door with all his might. Trying to figure out how to keep the hatch shut, James looked for anything heavy he could use as a barricade. The room had barely any visibility, but he noticed the outline of a large wooden desk just a few feet from him. He quickly got up and made his way hastily towards the object. James grabbed the wooden desk in the middle and began to shove it across the floor. The metal rivets under the desk's thick wooden legs produce a loud screeching sound. To James' surprise, a bust of adrenaline-filled his entire body. He didn't even notice nor felt the pain in his leg; the thought of not seeing his family and dying in this place gave James the strength to move the heavy desk up against the door so it wouldn't open. The loud screeching sounds of the desk scraping across the floor made James paranoid.

He prayed that nothing would hear the noise. Making sure not to be seen through the glass in the middle of the door, James crouched down as he pushed the desk right up against the door. Once the task was finished James moved as far away from the door as he could.

The darkness of the room provided him with a bit of cover as he crawled his way toward the back wall of the room. His eyes were now glued to the door like a kid watching their favorite cartoon show. In a matter of seconds, the mist outside had fully covered the entire hallway. James' hands were clammy and wet with sweat as his heart beat faster with fear. It felt as if it were about to burst forth from his chest.

Bullets of sweat poured from his face. He stared at the small window in the middle of the door, praying that whatever was out there couldn't hear the loud thumping of his heart beating, like a high school bass drum at a football game. As he watched, four long nail-like claws appeared from out of the mist. They began scraping the glass, making a loud, ear-piercing shriek. The pale, almost porcelain face of his pursuer pressed up against the glass. The noise was so unbearable that James was forced to put his hands over his ears. The racket lasted what felt like forever, but, as quickly as the darkness appeared, it vanished as if it were never there.

"What the hell was that?" James whispered. "That didn't look human at all." The nails looked to be at least eight inches long, charcoal black with dried blood on them. The fingers looked even longer still; they were thin, almost as if they were made of bone. The apparition didn't appear to feature any eyes. James continued to watch the door. "I think I am going to stay here for a minute or two longer."
After a few minutes of sitting in one spot, James hauled himself to his feet and unblocked the door. He poked his head out the entrance as he looked left, then right.

He expected to see whatever the thing was lurking nearby. After making sure it was clear, James stepped out of the room and now found himself back in the hallway. As James continued to make his way down the corridor, he suddenly heard what sounded like the static crackling on an old-fashioned grade school loudspeaker. About a minute later a male's voice soon began to resonate. "Hello. Hello? Is this thing on?"

"What? is somebody else also trapped in this place?" James burst out in confusion.

"Hello? Is anybody out there?" shouted the voice once more.

A tear escaped from James' eye. "Yes... Yes, I am here. I'm on the fifth floor!" James shouted, walking to an old tan, dusty speaker box hanging on the wall just a few feet from him. "Are you there? I know you're there," the man said. "I can see you in the surveillance system."

"Surveillance system?" James muttered, puzzled. He was taken back a bit by the words he had just heard. James started looking around the hallway for a camera. There, directly above the loudspeaker, was a small, almost unseen dome camera. *Oh shit. Can he see me? He did say he could see me. I'm saved.* "Hello, my name is James Callaway. I am a lawyer at Hunter, Schmitt, Mote & Associates law firm. I was kidnapped and put in this place. Can you help me?" yelled James at the camera as he waved his right arm.

"I just wanted to let you know that I have with me a very beautiful mother and her very beautiful daughter. They're here with me in this room tied up," The man said over the speaker as his tone began to change.

Wait, what did he just say? James was shocked and horrified. *He is not here to rescue me. He must have been the one to put me in this place, or he helped put me here. Now he has a mother and daughter tied up in this place? I can't imagine what he's planning on doing to them. I have to do something. I have to save them. If this were my family I would want someone in my place trying to save them. I would never forgive myself if I didn't do something to help them.*

"Before I am done playing with them, I will take the blade that is in my hand and cut their pretty little throats wide open. I will watch as the blood pours out of their necks like a beautiful crimson waterfall," the voice said in a cheerful demeanor. The tone of his speech was like that of a deranged psychopath. "But let's have some fun first. I think I'll start first with the daughter. Oh, my, she looks young, too, I'll say looks to be about thirteen, fourteen, maybe fifteen? Come on sweetheart, how old are you?"
The voice grew deep and raspy. "Why aren't you talking, little one? Oh, I know, it's because of my disgusting, ragged beard, isn't it? Well, don't worry, I'll make sure to wash out the lice and other bugs crawling around in it once I'm done with you and your mother. I will wash it nice and clean with the blood I collect from you two." James could almost hear the sick, wide smile on the man's face protruding through his ungroomed beard as has he walked up to the girl.

James made his way down the hall as quickly as he could. *Did I just hear him right? The young girl with him is about thirteen years old. That is the same age Amber is now. This fucking asshole is going to die. Don't you DARE lay a hand on her!* James' thoughts were now filled with pure anger as he imagined the mother and child being his wife and daughter. He proceeded down the hallway, trying to find the prison where they were being held.

"Say, princess, I have some fun planned for you," the man said over the speaker system. The mother tried to beg the guy to leave her daughter alone but she couldn't speak as her mouth was gagged. "Wait for your fucking turn, bitch," he told the mother as he slapped her across her face. James pictured the man just then running the back of his rough hand up and down the daughter's left cheek. "Oh, don't cry little one, this will be so much fun, I promise," he said to the girl. "You have very soft skin, young one. Nice and smooth."

James pictured in his mind the man continuing to gently caress the young girl's cheek. The girl shut her eyes tight in terror, trying to imagine that she was somewhere else. The girl was attempting to pretend this was all a nightmare. Yet she still felt the guy's rough, calloused hand caressing her skin.

"You see, they all called me insane and tossed me in here all because after playing with my toys I would cut them up and hang certain parts of them on my wall as mementos," the man said this to the girl while looking at her young, developed chest. Frustrated that her eyes were closed, he grabbed the young girl by her lower jaw. "Look at me you little bitch," he screamed as he slapped her across the face. The young girl's eyes bolted open with shock and fear as water formed began to stream down her cheeks. "That's a good girl," he said as he flashed his knife back forth across her face. The young girl's eyes grew wide with fear. She followed the knife going back and forth, left to right. "Let's have some fun, shall we?" he said as he took his blade and slowly started to pop the buttons one by one from her pink blouse. One by one, each of the buttons fell to the dark, hard stone floor as he cut them off. Once he was finished removing the buttons on the girl's blouse, he then violently ripped the garment off of her.

"Mmm... nice bra, does mommy knows that her little girl wears slutty shit like this?" he asks. The man took his knife and removed the young girl's black laced bra. The teenager was deathly terrified as her eyes darted to lock with her mother's, both pairs filled with fear.

"Well, well, I can see where you inherited your mother's great genes. Your tits are so soft and perky and just about as big as dear old mom's, I would say." The man grabbed the teen's now-fully exposed chest. A large bulge began to grow down his left leg as he continued to grope her breast. "I haven't had the pleasure of feeling the soft, smooth flesh of a teenage girl in a very long time," he told her as he continued to grope her bosoms. Tears raced down her face as she looked at the man continued to feel his way around her. She held nothing but pure fear in her eyes. The man was delighted in having his way with her.

"I... I have to get to them before this psycho takes it any further. But where the hell are they?" yelled James in frustration as he came to a three-way split in the middle of the hall. "I have no idea what path to take now or what I will do when I find him. But I can't just stand here and listen to what is taking place. It's just downright sickening, even horrifying." James could now hear what sounded like muffled crying along with heavy breathing coming from the speaker that was closest to him. He tried hard not to imagine what awful things the guy was doing to the teenager. "You leave her the fuck alone you bastard!" James yelled into the microphone before running down the path to his right, the path he believed would take him to whatever chamber the mother and daughter was been held at.

"I bet your boyfriend will be so very jealous of you once he finds out that you had another guy's dick inside you," the voice of the man told the young girl with a smile on his face as he unzipped his pants, exposing his hard, nearly ten-inch long member to the young girl. Her eyes widened in shock as she stared at his cock.

"This... this is not right. Someone has to put a stop this. Please, someone, stop it!" James screamed as he raced towards where he believed the mother and daughter were being held, hoping that someone else was in the building and that they could also hear what was happening. As he trotted the halls, his leg gave out and collapsed out from under him, forcing James to once again fall hard onto the grime-encrusted floor. "Damn it!" James cried out as he pounded his fist hard on the floor, knowing that there was nothing he can do to help the two women. He sat there as tears ran down his face. Then the muffled crying stopped. "Did he? Oh, God... please, no." James said aloud as his mouth and eyes widening with fear. "Please, God, don't let her be dead." All James could picture at that moment in his head was his own daughter, Amber. He could see his little princess being brutally raped and then killed, lying naked on the cold, dark floor, covered in a pool of her own blood.

The man passed the bloody knife back and forth across the dead girl's face, smearing her own blood across her cheeks. He then walked over to the mother, who was now raging furiously at what she had just witnessed happening to her child.

The woman attempted breaking free of her restraints but, try as she might, she was thoroughly unsuccessful. The lunatic just stood still a couple of feet in front of her, watching her struggle, with a grin splashed over his face. He then swiftly grabbed the mother by her neck, nearly choking the life out of her. "You're feisty; I like that in a woman," he calmly told her as he removed the gag from her mouth before kissing her on the lips. He then began the whole process once more, doing to the woman the same thing as he did to her child. The man took his knife and cut both her shirt and bra off, exposing the woman's well-developed breasts.

"Oh, my! Your tits are so much bigger than your dead daughters were," he said to her.

"Fuck you," the mother told him, spitting in his face, trying to fight him off. The rope that bound her to the chair was loosened and slipped down a bit. "So much spunk in you," the lunatic said. "I think it's time that I teach who's the fucking boss around here you colossal bitch." He punched her in the face several times. Blood now trickled down from her broken nose and busted lip.

The man untied the woman from the chair and began to drag her along the ground by her long, reddish tint hair. She kept trying to fight him off while screaming at him to let her go. Suddenly, the man picked her up from the ground and slammed her hard onto the wooden desk before them. He then forced the mother to turn over on her stomach and struck her in the back of her head, causing her to lose consciousness for a moment.

While she was limp, spread over the desk, face down and unconscious, he retied the woman onto the desk. He tied both of her legs spread out wide to the lower part of the desk, as well as her arms across the top of the furniture. The mother, now coming out of her haze, realized what had just happened to her. Trying to lift herself on her feet, she soon realized that she was tied down. Her eyes grew wide as a look of pure dread blanketed her face.

“Hey, out there, I hope you are listening. Are you ready for the main event? It’s going to be a scream!” the depraved lunatic screeched over the mic, with a grin on his face, as he ripped off the woman’s pants and underwear. He then began to rape her just like he did to the young girl. Loud, crying screams were heard throughout the entire building, along with heavy breathing and even some moaning.

All James could do was sit there and just listen to what this guy was doing. He couldn’t muster up the strength to get off of the floor. James kept picturing in his mind that the unknown women were his wife and daughter that were tied up in the room. The guy untied the mother from the desk and then forced her to her hands and knees. He proceeded to rape her once more. Thoroughly broken, the woman was now on the ground on all fours as if she were some kind of dog. She closed her eyes tight, crying in silence as she could feel him inside of her. The pain of his member pulsating each time he thrust deeper made her whimper even more. After what felt like an eternity he finally pulled out of her. She could feel the hot thickness of his semen oozing out of her now-bleeding rectum. The mixture of bodily fluids ran down her legs as if it were a waterfall.

The crazed man then forcefully shoved his member, covered in blood and fecal matter, down her throat, forcing her to swallow more of his hot, thick load as he came again and again. She tried to pull away but he held her head in place as he fucked her throat. "Ahh... that was great, bitch," the man said as he pulled out of her mouth.
He took out his knife and pressed it up against the woman's throat. Her eyes grew wide with fear. "Please don't kill me," she begged of him as she cried.

Smiling at her, the man began wrapping her hair around his hand. Forcefully pulling the back of her hair, yanking her neck back as he looked in her in the eyes. "You know what my favorite song in the world was growing up? That still plays in my head non- stop on repeat." He asked her. The woman was too paralyzed with fear to answer. "Here: I'll sing it to you!" the man told her, filled with unadulterated glee, as he continued to peer into her eyes.

"You are my sunshine, my only sunshine. You make me happy... when skies are gray."

As he slowly voiced each note of the song, he pressed the dull blade of the knife against her throat. The mother's eyes grew wider as she tried to scream but couldn't as no words would escape out of her mouth. The blade then began to penetrate the skin of her throat.

"You'll never know dear, how much I loved you. So, please, don't take my sunshine away."

As the man continued singing his song, he slowly sank the blade very deep across her throat, slicing it wide open. Within mere seconds, blood began to run down her neck like the Hoover Dam itself was bursting forth from the seams. As he finished singing the song, her body grew cold, limp, and soon fell to the floor.

"I must find them... I have to find them... I have to save them," James wept to himself as he got back to his feet. He was determined to save the mother and daughter. If not save them, then the least he could do was tell the police which room the bodies were in so that their family could give them a proper burial. Gathering his courage, James proceeded to make his way as fast as he could down the hall. As he approached the end of the hallway, James noticed a door just a few feet in front of him. The writing on the door read, *Main Office. 502.* "This must be the room?" he asked himself in a low tone. James walked up to the door, placing the right side of his face against it. Pressing his ear hard on the cold metal, James could hear the man's voice inside the room, still maniacally laughing.

James then looked into the room through the small plexiglass window. He could see an older white man, about 5 ft 8 inches. The man was wearing old, tattered clothes that looked as if they hadn't been washed in years. This man had a long, ungroomed, graying beard. James could also see two bodies lying on the ground.
The light of the hall couldn't give him the full detail of who they belong to but James knew that they were dead. He took a deep breath.

"I've got you now you fucking asshole!" shouted James, not knowing what was waiting for him on the other side of the door. James barged in the room; he was ready for a fight. James was ready for something, anything. But inside there he found nothing. The room was almost completely empty except for a long counter, a few broken chairs with dust and cobwebs covering them, and a wooden desk with a mic on it. There were zero signs of the man or of the dead bodies of the two women lying naked on the cold hard ground. It was as if the crazed, deranged, psychotic killer was never there to begin with. Neither were the two victims of his rampage, for that matter.

"What the hell is going on? I know that this was the room. I heard his voice from behind the door. I even saw him and the bodies of the mother and her daughter!" said James, confused. "I know I must be going crazy. I know what I've seen. I know I just saw them!" James told himself.

Puzzled at what just happened, James quickly turned around and headed back down the hallway. Halfway down the corridor, his right leg gave out, causing him to once again hit the cold, hard floor. As he laid in the filth covering the pearly white tiles, James could still hear the blade of the knife slicing through each layer of skin of the mother's throat and the gurgling sounds she made as her blood bubbled and poured out of her neck. "I... I couldn't save them. I couldn't save them," James kept quietly repeating to himself as he started to sob, laying on the ground. His legs now pressed against his chest and his head was now buried between his folded knees. James just kept on repeating, "I'm sorry, I'm sorry." After a little while, James closed his eyes and began to think of his wife and daughter and how worried and scared they must be right now. He contemplated deeply about how much he missed them.

CHAPTER 5

"Daddy, Daddy, are you ready?" a little girl's voice ranged out asking with excitement in her voice. "Ready? Ready for what?" James asked as he opened his eyes to see a bright-eyed little girl with big, green eyes and wild, bright blonde hair looking right at him.

"To go to the park today! You promised me that you would take me and mommy to the park today."

"Did I say today?" James asked of his daughter, pretending as if he had forgotten.

"Yeah, Daddy, you did!" Amber replied with a sour look.

"I did say that we would go to the park today, huh? Okay, my little angel, run upstairs and get ready, okay?" James told his daughter with a broad smile across his face.

"Yeah! We're going to the park! I have the best Daddy ever!" shouted Amber as she raced up the stairs to her bedroom. She was wearing her favorite pajamas and her hair was wild and matted. James got up out of bed, still wearing just his boxers. He threw on a t-shirt and walked downstairs into the kitchen. He grabbed some Starbucks coffee grinds, a clean pot, and set a mug nearby on the kitchen counter. The mug was shaped like an owl, with a ceramic baby owl set inside it on the bottom. It was the previous year's Christmas gift from his wife. After a few minutes, coffee brewed, he sat down at the kitchen table with his wife Liz, who had just walked into the kitchen after waking up. "Well done, dad," she tells her husband as she kissed him on the left cheek.

"Well, I did promise her that we would go to the park today. Besides, she won't be five forever," James replied while sipping from the rim of his mug.

"No, she won't," Liz replied as she walked over to the coffee pot and poured a fresh cup coffee into her white porcelain mug. On the side of it was emblazoned Best Wife Ever along with a cartoon heart.

"Well we have a few minutes," Liz told her husband seductively as she slowly sipped on her coffee. "How about we go to the bedroom and pick out our clothes?" Liz held a seductive smile upon her face as she put her coffee mug down and walked out of the kitchen. She was wearing her low-cut black t-shirt and sexy red laced silk boxer shorts. James' eyes grew wide with lust as he watched his wife pull down her boxers a tad to tease him a bit by showing off her silky smooth, sexy ass. Not enough to fully show; just enough to turn him on. James took one big gulp of his coffee and promptly put down the mug to chase his wife upstairs. A few minutes later, they both got dressed and went downstairs where Amber was waiting for them on the couch.

"Hey, Amber, are you ready?" Liz asked her.

"Oh, yes, mommy, I am!" Amber squealed to her mom while sitting on the short, dark brown couch watching the morning cartoons on TV. "Hey, mom," shouted Amber, "are you making lunch for us to bring to the park?" Amber asked.

"No, your dad said we will pick up something on the way, okay?" Liz was in the process of fixing her already perfect hair in the mirror by the door.

"Okay, mom," Amber replied, eyes still fixed on the cartoons. Liz grabbed her tan leather purse and yelled, "Well, James, we're ready. Amber, turn the TV off, please." Amber got up from the couch and flipped the television switch. She placed the remote down on the glass coffee table and walked to the door.

James strutted down the stairs and stopped on the second step from the bottom, staring in awe at how beautiful his wife and daughter looked. Liz was wearing a nice, light blue button-down short-sleeve shirt and dark blue jean pants with her black Reeboks on. Her somewhat long autumn brown hair was pulled into a ponytail. Amber had on her pink and red Minnie Mouse dress which was pretty well worn down. The red of the dress was faded into an almost pink along with several small rips. She also had on her favorite pink pants which looked more like high waters as well as her light up shoes. She also wore several different braids in her long blonde hair.

"Okay, are we all ready to go to the park?" James asked his family with sheer delight in his voice.

"Yes, I'm ready!" Amber shouted back with glee.

"Ok then, hop in the car," Liz told her.

James' car was an old '87 black Thunderbird. It was passed down from his dad to James when he passed away. The car has a few dents and scratches, and the upholstery in the inside was changed once or twice, but the vehicle still ran great. Amber loved messing with the old cassette tape player that her grandpa had installed in it.
She brought her best friend, Mr. Bear Bear, along for the ride. "Ok Mr. Bear Bear, Daddy is about to drive, so we must put our set belt on," she told her stuff best friend as she clicked the belt. James looked into the rear-view mirror.

“Okay, are we all buckled up?” he asked as he started the car. Amber just looked at him and smiled. Liz rested her hand on his arm as they backed out of the driveway and set off for the park.

After about twenty minutes on the road, they stopped at a fast-food drive-thru. Liz asked Amber what she would like to eat. “Chicken nuggets!” Amber gleefully replied while looking out the car window. “Okay, so one chicken nugget kids’ meal, and I’ll have a dressed hamburger with small fries,” Liz told James as she dug into her purse for some money.

“Okay,” replied James as he drove the car up to the speaker box. “Hello and welcome to Dairy Queen, would you like to try our new triple chocolate brownie shake today?” the young female voice asked. James looked at Amber and Liz for a second. “Yes,” he replied. Relaying his beloved ladies’ orders to the speaker, James added, “I would also like a double bacon burger with a small order of fries, as well as three medium-size chocolate brownie shakes. “Okay,” the cashier said as she repeated the order back to him. “Yes, that is correct,” James told her. “That will be eighteen dollars and eleven cents, please pull up to the second window.”

A few moments later, after they received their food, the family was back on the road heading towards the park. It took them about another half-hour to reach their destination. Amber quickly unbuckled her seatbelt and got out of the car.

“Yay, the park. Come on, Mr. Bear Bear!” she burst out loud as she ran for the swings. “Amber, we have to eat first” Liz shouted after her daughter as she and James grabbed the food out of the car. They walked up to the nearest picnic table next to the swing sets.

The table itself was old fashioned; it was constructed from wood and painted red, with plenty of teenage names and boasts carved onto its' surface from over the years. The three of them sat down and began eating. "Daddy, mommy, can we pick some flowers to bring home, please?" Amber asked while eating a nugget. "Yeah, love, we can pick some flowers to bring home," Liz replied.

"Thanks, mom. I'm done, dad; can me and Mr. Bear Bear go and play now?"

"Yes, of course. You and Mr. Bear Bear can go play; just be careful." James told her while finishing his meal. Amber got up and ran towards the swing set as fast as she could with her stuffed teddy bear hanging in tow.
"This was a good idea," Liz told her husband as she sipped her milkshake.

"Yeah, it was, huh? It was a good idea to come here. The air feels so nice and cool, the sun is out, it's nice and warm and the trees look great." James and Liz watched their daughter play. "Yeah, it is a great day." James walked over to the nearby wastebasket and disposed of the family's trash.

"Oh, hey, hun, I heard from Paul's wife Margret."

"Paul? I haven't seen him since the day I had my first big case" James replied to Liz.

A few hours later, James stood up from the table, turned around, and started to walk over to the car. He was thinking about his old friend Paul. Liz called Amber from the swings. "James, James, hey, James." A voice called from behind him. James closed his eyes for a brief moment.

CHAPTER 6

"Hey man, ready for your big day?" Paul asked James. "Yeah, ready as I'll ever be." They were both walking down the hall toward the elevator. "Well, I hope you are, man. No more small court cases for you, huh? You're in the big leagues now." Paul was looking at the time on the watch adorning his left wrist. Along with his watch, he wore a normal black suit with a white shirt and red tie. His blond hair was neatly combed to the right. Paul was tall and thin. James had on a dark gray suit, white shirt, blue tie as well as a black digital watch on his right wrist. "Nope, no more small cases for me," James told his long-time friend and colleague. "This case will either make or break my career. So, I have to go into the courtroom and convince the jury that my client is innocent. Easy, right?" James nervously told Paul as the pair got onto the elevator. "What floor James?" Paul asked as he had already pushed number ten. "Oh, floor eight please, Paul," James replied, checking his pager. Paul pressed the corresponding button.

"Hey, how is Liz doing these days?"

"Great. We are about to have our first baby," James excitedly told Paul.

"Congratulations, man! So, do y'all know what sex of the baby will be?"

"Yes, we found out the other day, in fact. We're having a little girl. Liz and I have already decided on the name Amber."

“Amber, huh? Lovely name,” Paul said as he congratulated James again. The elevator continued its’ slow climb upward. The soft instrumental music of jazz played on repeat as the two friends talked a bit more.

“Hey Paul, do you know anything about this judge, O’Connor?” James asked, trying to find out what kind of judge he'll be working with.

“You have Justice O’Connor?” Paul replied with an eyebrow raised.

“Yeah, do you know anything about her?”

“Why, yes, I do,” said Paul. “Justice Raven O’Connor. Her nickname around the courthouse is the madhouse judge. She is extremely hard to work with and obsessively goes by the book. You don’t want to fuck around with this judge, James.”

The two of them spent the rest of the elevator ride in silence. James knew a little bit about Justice O’Connor already. He knew that she was a small but feisty woman. No taller than five feet. Her hair was short, curly, and jet black. Justice O’Connor wore small, red-rimmed glasses that hugged the bridge of her nose. The nearly sixty-year-old made a name for herself by putting ninety-eight percent of all people who were charged with something behind bars. She even sentenced a law enforcement veteran of twenty-three years to prison because he ended up crippling the black suspect he had been chasing after. The only time James had ever seen her before was on TV; that particular case held a very profile given the city’s ongoing racial tensions.

“I am at awe that your first real case as a lawyer is held in front of her, but, please man, tread carefully with her. I’ve heard too many stories that lawyers fall quiet after dealing with her,” Paul told his friend before James was exiting the elevator, concerned.

"Well, my client is a twenty-seven-year-old white male who the district attorney alleges murdered a man. So, I have to do what I can to convince judge and jury that he is innocent." James listened as the elevator's alarm sounded, sending a body impeding the closing of its' door. Paul just looked at James before finally conceding, "Well, good luck man." "Thanks, Paul," James replied as walked out of the elevator sensor's path. Walking away, he took a glance back to see that the silver doors of the elevator had closed. As James walked down the hall he came up to the large, dark mahogany wooded door that marked his destination. Okay, James, you got this, he told himself as he took a deep breath. He grabbed the silver-gold finished door handle that laid before him. As James opened the door the bright lights of the room engulfed his vision.

James entered the courtroom. The small, public area in the back was filled with people; family members of both the defendant and deceased, as well as steely-eyed court reporters and curious onlookers. James walked down the aisle and began to look around the room. Twelve jurors were sitting on the right-hand side of the room, near the judge's bench. The jury itself was a mixture of men and women; old and young; white, black, and mixed in between. The audience section of the room, which seats about eighty, looked to be composed of a similar mixture. James made his way to his desk where he was greeted by a young lady named Zoie Staples.

"Hello. I'm Zoie. You must be James." The lady shook offered her hand, and James shook it in turn, "Yes, of course, so I am," he replied. "So, you're here to-"

"Help," Zoie said, interrupting James mid-sentence. James looked at her, taken back. "Ah, yes, help," he said as he placed his briefcase on the defendant's table. This desk itself already featured the neatly scattered papers from Zoie's law firm on this case, along with two small plastic cups and a pitcher of water.

“I am from the Greene, Carew & Belisle law firm, as you probably already know. Hunter, Schmitt, Mote & Associates contacted my firm and asked if we could help.” She told this to James while semi-frantically shifting through her papers. James sat down and opened up his briefcase, pulling out his own set of paperwork. The bailiff entered the room; a well-built, middle-aged black male. He was clean-shaven and about 6 ft tall even. The uniform he wore was a tan, short sleeve buttoned shirt with his name embroidered above his left breast pocket, with the badge of the city police department above his right. He also had on navy blue pants, shirt neatly tucked in. Around his waist was the standard-issue utility belt; James particularly admired the bailiff’s handgun as well as the sliver handcuffs that glimmered in the light.

“All rise for the Honorable Justice Raven O’Connor,” the bailiff boomed at the room with a severe tone. Immediately all in the room fell silent as everyone stood up. A moment after Justice O’Connor came out of her chambers, she sat down in her chair. “You may all be seated,” the bailiff once again broadcast in the loud tone. “Thank you, Brandon,” Justice O’Connor replied, in a calm voice unbefitting her fierce reputation. “Okay, Brandon, what do we have on the docket today?” The bailiff walked up to the bench and gave the judge a small stack of papers. As he was handing over the paperwork, two officers city officers, similarly dressed as the bailiff, brought forward a middle-aged white male. He wore an orange jumpsuit with the numbers in bold that read *8901109* on his top right breast pocket. He was of average height, a freshly shaped scalp with a handful of razor-burn bumps, and a tiny amount of facial hair that could faintly pass for a beard. The officer placed the man in a chair right next to Zoie and James.

"Case number *37561*, The State versus Adam Bridgewater. Mr. Bridgewater is accused by The State of the murder in the first degree of one Tommy Silkwood, on the date of Monday the 23rd of October. Today we are here to set trial. How does the defendant plea?" Justice O'Connor asked while looking at Adam. "Not guilty, your honor," Zoie replied while standing up.

James took control over the proceedings. "Your honor. Mr. Bridgewater only killed one Tommy Silkwood out of self-defense. As he said in this testimony statement that I will now read aloud to the courtroom. Please note that this is Adam Bridgewater's own words as it was recorded."

"Quote, 'I did not mean to kill Tommy Silkwood. He came toward me and my girlfriend with a knife while we were at my home. I only tried to subdue him. This killing will forever haunt me for the rest of my days. No words can express how sorry I am for his family.'

You see, Mr. Bridgewater did not murder Tommy out of an act of hate or even jealousy but rather in self-defense, and by accident, remind you." James said as he looked at the jury. The case went on back and forth for a good nine hours with few breaks in between. The jury listened to both the defense and prosecution and took copious amounts of notes, then recessed for another two to deliberate on a verdict. After the last recess, the bailiff asked for everyone to please rise for the judge. Justice Raven O'Connor came back out and everyone once again took their seats.

"Okay, it is 7:45 pm. I hope that the jury has had enough time to reach a verdict?" She asked them. "Yes, your honor." one of the jurors stated, the head of the jury. "We the People of the jury find the defendant Adam Bridgewater guilty of the murder of the first degree of Tommy Silkwood."

Just then Adam bolted up out of his seat screaming, “No!” The two officers quickly grabbed Adam by the arms. “I will have silence in my court!” Justice O’Connor said in a loud, firm tone as she banged her gavel three times on desk; each strike was harder than the last. James and Zoie both looked at their client as the two cops had him retained near the door he’d emerged from earlier in the day.

“Please, continue,” the judge said after her courtroom was back in order. The head juror cleared his throat and proceeded with the verdict. After the decision was read, Justice O’Connor made her final speech before telling Adam of his sentence. “Mr. Bridgewater, the court has found you guilty of the murder of Tommy Silkwood. I hereby sentence you to the maximum life in prison in the State Penitentiary with no chance for parole. This is my final decision. I thank all the jurors and everybody who was a part of this case. Please drive home safely.” Justice O’Connor told the courtroom. A loud outburst of cursing and threats rang out in the courtroom as Adam was now going ballistic. “I’m innocent, damn it, I’m innocent!” He then looked at James; his eyes were full of rage and hate as he yelled at his lawyer. “You fucking liar, you told me that you would get me off, you told me that you were the fucking best. Fuck you, you fucking asshole. I’ll get you back for this James, I’ll get out and I’ll make you pay. Even if I have to kidnap your God damn family, you hear me!” shouted Adam.

James just looked on in a state of shock as his first case crumbled before him. He was so numb to his surroundings that he did not process what Adam was shouting. He just stood there as one by one the people left the courtroom. The bailiff, Brandon, walked over to James. “Hey Mister, the court is closing; time to go home.” Brandon shook James’ right shoulder. “Mister, hello, Mister, time to go.” He told James this one more time as he shined his flashlight into the young lawyer’s face. A bright light engulfed James’ vision.

CHAPTER 7

James woke up from his daydream to the pain of a large black rat gnawing on the flesh of his left hand. "Ahhh! Mother fucker," he screamed, batting the rat away from his fingers. James could still feel the burning, stinging pain in his hand where the rat had bitten him hard. Blood rose to the top of his hand, drowning the loose, ripped flesh as it ran down the top of his left hand onto the ground. "My family," James muttered emotionally. He ripped off a lower piece of his shirt and wrapped it around the bleeding, gaping hole in his left hand. As James was holding the now-blood soaked rag tightly against his hand, he began to think to himself. *I need to stay focused. I can't let my mind become broken in this place. I have to find a way out of this hell so I can see my family again. I need to be able to hold them again. I want so much to hold both Amber and Liz in my arms so badly and tell them how much I love them. But first, I must find a way out.* He grabbed his cane and placed it under his right hand. James then pulled himself back to his feet using both the wall and the cane. He decided to search the room for a clue or a hint that could help him out.

The room was a mess. Old wires were hanging from the ceiling; some were cut and scattered all over the ground. The wooden desk in the center of the room looked fragile. The wooden legs that held up the desk looked as if they could give way at any moment, as did the rest of the desk. On the desk was an old microphone system and a switch that was covered in thick, grayish dust. *Huh. This must have been the room that lunatic used for those announcements.* Flashbacks of the deranged lunatic raping the mother and daughter came back to him while he was rummaging through the desk drawers.

The room had a smell to it that reminded one of a sewer treatment plant. The pungent odor filled the air of room like a scented candle.

As James continued to dig around in the drawers his left hand started to hurt even more. “God damn it, fucking rat,” he shouted in anger. “It’s bad enough that my right leg is messed up and that I have a hole in my head the size of a half-dollar. I’m now losing more blood thanks to that fucking rat. Now I’m missing a chunk out of my left hand because a fucking rat decided that my hand was its’ fucking dinner. Ah, my head feels fuzzy with everything that’s going on. I have to see if there’s a map of this building so I can see what floor the medical ward was on. Maybe if I find that area, I might be able to find a first aid kit.” James looked through all of the drawers in the room. All he kept finding were old papers and letters that have aged with time. One of the papers James had just found in a lower file cabinet drawer along the wall caught his eye.

The writing looked as if an inmate wrote it or, at least, a very rushed staff member. The paper, just like the rest, was old with a brownish-yellow tint to it. As James picked up the paper to bring it to the hallway to read it crumpled into dust right there in his hand.

“Well, that’s just fucking great,” he sighed out, disappointed. “I have searched this entire fucking room and still I’ve found nothing that will help me out.” James shook his head in frustration as he exited the room. Back in the hallway, he felt an odd feeling roll over him again. It felt almost as if someone, or something, was following him. “Nah... it’s nothing,” James tried to tell himself. “It’s this place; this damn place is messing with my head. Come on, James, get a grip.” James stood under the dim light wiping the tiredness from his eyes from lack of sleep.

As he made his way down the corridor, he soon came across what looked to be another entrance to an unexplored hallway. This passage seemed different than the previous ones. The ceiling was made to appear like a large stone arch. It looked as if three large wooden beams were holding it together. The wood was painted an off-white color, but time had taken its' toll. The paint was cracked and peeling away from the beams. The hallway was so dark that it made it difficult for James to peer down.

The more James stared down the darkness of the hallway, the more he felt a sinister presence peering back toward him. In a spilt second, James swore he had seen two glowing, reddish-yellow eyes in the dark staring at him. Shaken, James quickly turned and left from the spot in which he was standing and hurried to the other hallway. "What the hell was that back there? Did I just see what I thought I saw, or has the lack of blood, food, and rest finally taken effect over me?" James asked himself. "I bet Liz must be pissed at me for not calling her." James came up to the stairway door.

Okay, I need to find some medical supplies fast before I collapse for good. I'm guessing that the first floor may have a map posted concerning layout to this place. Maybe I can grab a first aid kit and get the fuck out of here.

As James slowly walked down the stairs to the first floor, he felt a very strong gust of cold wind rushing past him. James quickly looked all around to see where this freezing breeze may have originated from. As he was standing on one of the concrete steps in the middle of the stairway, James unconsciously looked up ahead of himself. He gazed just in time to watch the heavy metal door suddenly slam shut. James rubbed his eyes in disbelief as he thought he had just seen what looked to be a shadow or hand on the door before it closed.

Too nervous and scared to go see what it the apparition may have been, James now hastily walked down the stairs. After what seemed to be forever, James reached the bottom of the stairway. The sign above the door stated *First Floor.* "Thank God!" James exclaimed as he caught his breath.

CHAPTER 8

As James slowly opened the pale, gray metal door, he noted that the first floor was different from the other levels he had encountered. The hallway was still a muck disaster but he could make out the black and white checkered pattern tiles covering the floor. James began to walk down the long corridor. The first floor featured fewer rooms than any of the other levels of the building; James counted only three doors here. *This will make searching for the medical ward a lot easier,* James thought. As he walked the passage, he began to realize that there was more light Illuminating the hallway than he'd previously encountered on other floors. The extra lighting that was shining in this hallway, it turned out, was emanating from the moon. Lunar beams were coming through the painted windows on the right-hand side of the corridor. This light shining down from outside came as a bit of comfort to James. He could see a bit better now than he could before than with the dim flickering lights on the previous floors. The shadows that the moonlight cast was not as creepy as the ones produced by the yellowed hanging fixtures.

Strange, James thought as he began to examine the window next to him. *Why are there iron bars on the outside window frame? Was it to keep the patients from escaping?* The more he stared at the iron bars, the more he began to notice why there was no moonlight to be found shining upon the other floors. James looked out the window towards what he figured to be the west wing of the hospital. James could see then that a massive cluster of dark brown vines had overtaken the entire building. The wild plants had encased the entire front of the hospital from the second floor on up, including all of the windows.

As James moved away from the window, he caught a better glimpse of the doors at the end of the hallway. *One of those doors must be the medical ward. If I'm right, then that is where I will find what I need to help fix my damaged leg and my head along with my other injuries.* James started inching his way toward those doors. With each step that James took to bring himself closer to these doors, the pain in his leg increased. *This would have never happened if I had just left work early, he tried to tell himself as he fought through the pain. I would be at home with my wife and daughter this very minute watching TV, no doubt eating some unhealthy junk food.* James used the wall as extra leverage to help him walk. The old cream-color paint that once coved the walls were now peeling away, falling towards the ground in various sized chunks. A line of what looks like ashes laid alongside the wooden baseline of the floor.

Large, deep cracks ran along both sides of the walls in an upward zig-zag pattern toward the ceiling with a handful of peeling paint chunks barely hanging on. He could see the stained wooden beams protruding through holes in the walls with the help of the extra light.

As James got closer to the center of the hallway, he noticed a very strange door that looked to lead directly outside. "What the fuck is that?" James asked himself aloud as he fixed his gaze onto the large metal door. This door could be seen through the glass walls that separated the entrance and the waiting room. The waiting room was a complete mess; there were outdated magazines scattered about along with some random bits of trash and carcasses of dead rats. These bodies strewn about the floor were being eaten by roaches and fly larvae. The waiting room also had missing and broken chairs. "I bet that door will get me out of this damn place," James said to himself as he noticed what looked to be the help desk. Just a few feet away, to the right, was a door leading behind the reception area.

Before I go and check that room, let me see if there is a key I can use to open the strange metal door. Maybe I can use it to get the fuck out of here. James approached the reception desk.

The desk was just like all the others James had seen in the hospital. It was wooden and covered with dust and cobwebs, as well as some papers scattered on top. *Well, this is not a big surprise to me,* thought James as he began searching inside the drawers. The first two contained nothing of importance to him inside them but, as James looked inside the third drawer, he found an old silver ring with several keys attached to it. “Yes! Keys! I can now open that weird door an get the fuck out of here!” exclaimed James excitedly as a smile absorbed his face. Without a second thought, James grabbed the keys. “Oh, I can’t wait to see my little girl and my beautiful wife and hold both of them in my arms once more.” He raced as fast as he could toward the metal door. When James reached the door he immediately began searching for the keyhole. The lock on this door was oddly different than any of the other locks found throughout the hospital. Just then, James realized just how different this door was from all the others; this door did not feature a keyhole like a normal door but instead, it had an eight digital numeric number lock. “Fucking great!” shouted James in frustration as he punched the metal door. Upset, James walked back toward the help desk. In the door next to it was etched *Room 101.* Thankfully, this door was unlocked, and James entered the room. He was greeted with a cold chill that ran straight up his spine. *Someone must have been here because the door was open. Perhaps some college kids were in here looking to bust some ghosts.*

He stepped further into the room and began looking around. *This room is a mess. Nothing here but old, outdated paperwork. This is not the medical ward. I won’t find any medical supplies in here.* James felt upset. He thought about Liz and Amber to try keeping himself from going insane.

Obviously, this room was the filing room. All I can see scattered everywhere are financial documents and files on the patients, along with the check-in/check-out release forms. As James dug through the junk a bit more, he stumbled across an old leather notebook. *Why would something like this be here?* he thought as he skimmed through the pages of the notebook. While flipping through the book, James noticed a few pages had numbers circled in red ink. "This might be useful," he mused as he shoved the book in his left pants pocket. James was about to leave the room when he heard the scratching sounds of a rat clawing the wood underneath the desk.

"Huh? What was that?" James said as he moved the desk away from the wall. A small hole was punched in the drywall behind it. *I would have never realized that this was here if it had not been for the rat.* James stooped down, shoved his left arm into the small opening, and started digging around. After several minutes of rummaging through the hole, James felt something solid. He pulled out an old cassette player that somebody had hidden behind the desk. The cassette player was small and gray, with a red button for "record" and black buttons to play, rewind and fast forward. Inside the player was a cassette tape. James pulled it out and noted that on the tape's face, in black marker, the name *Kelly Mailhos* was written.

The device itself was covered in a thick layer of dust; nobody had apparently touched it in years. *A power cord can be attached to it, but, I have neither the cord nor power,* James thought to himself as he examined it closer. Popping open the back cover, James was relieved that there was still a set of batteries inside. "Let's hope they still work," James told the still air around him.

Before James played the tape, he reached his hand up the drywall one last time to see if anything else was there. After a little bit of rummaging, he pulled out a small piece of paper.

"What is this, now?" he said as he inspected it. The paper was black and folded; the texture reminded James of wax. He carefully unfolded the leaflet, trying not to damage it. A large drawing in white chalk outline began to slowly take shape. "This... this is the map of the hospital!"

James examined the map, now unfolded. "Where could the medical ward possibly be?" The large map was hand-drawn, with only the main rooms labeled. There it was; the medical ward, on the fifth floor, where James had already been. James shuddered as he remembered passing the location the map claimed it was located; he had felt eerie darkness emanating from that hallway. *Just my luck. Before I go back up there, let me first see what's recorded on the tape.* James sat down on the cold, hard floor and placed the small audiotape back inside the cassette player.
Pressing on the largest black button, the audio began to come to life. There were a few seconds of static at first; but then, just as James was about to shut the device off, a man's voice started speaking.

CHAPTER 9

"Testing. Testing. Hello, my name is Dr. Philip Brookside. I am the head psychiatrist here at St. Mary's Hospital. Today's date is October 28th, 1987. Today I will be recording the first of five audio sessions. The patient number: 0388901. The name: Kelly Mailhos.

Kelly is a 23-year-old female who suffers from acute psychosis. Her symptoms: Hysteria. Visual hallucination. Multiple personality disorder and false memories. Let's begin the session."

"Hello, Kelly," the doctor said as the patient entered the room. *"How are you doing today?"*

"Hi, Doctah Brookside, I doing good. Didja get a new sofa?"

"Yes, Kelly. I recently had the old sofa replaced with this new one right here in my office. It's very nice of you to notice."

"Well, Doctah B, I like it."

"Thank you, Kelly. Kelly, do you know why you are here?"

"Yeah. Is because I believe I seeing things that ain't there." Her southern accent was particularly thick. James wondered where she was originally from.

"That is right, Kelly. Is that why you're scanning the room right now, left and right? ... Note that the patient nodded affirmation. Okay, Kelly. Please keep in mind that while I am recording this session, I am also

writing everything down that you are telling me. Kelly, I would like you to lay down on the sofa and just look at the ceiling."

"Okay, Doctah B."

There was a brief pause in the audio; James heard a sofa squeak as, he presumed, the patient was adjusting herself on it.

"Great. Now, Kelly, just close your eyes and listen to the sound of the metronome." Another brief silence. Then came a clicking noise, along with the sounds of a pen tip scratching onto paper.
"Okay, Kelly. I am now going to count back from ten to one. When I get to one, you will be in a relaxed state, okay?"

"Okay, doctah."

There was a sound of ticking coming from the tape. The Doctor was speaking softly, now. *"Ten... nine... eight..."* Once Dr. Brookside reached one; there was another short pause, then he asked his patient, *"Are you still with me?"*

"Yes, Doctah. I am still with you." Her voice now sounded very relaxed.

"Okay, Kelly. Can you tell me about my office, please?"

"Yes, I can. There is... a large bookcase to the right of your desk. There are a few books on it, an' a bronze statue of a Spanish bull. Your desk got a picture of you an' your friend in a boat, fishing. You got a new black leather chair, and a new sofa."

"Very good, Kelly. ... Okay. Now, Kelly, I would like you to tell me about your friend."

Kelly's voice raised, almost as if she were in shock. *"Who? HIM?"*

"Yes, of course. Tell me about him." James could once again hear the sound of a pen scribbling onto paper, only this time, the writing was quick and steady.

"I don't... I don't think I can?" Kelly said as if it were a question, not a statement.

"Okay. Why don't you think you can tell me about him?"

"He will get mad at me," Kelly replied in a hushed, child-like whisper. James had to stop and rewind once to relisten because her voice was so low.

"Has he been mad at you before?"

"He..." James could picture this girl tearing up in his mind. *"He hurt my family."*

"He hurt your family? How did he hurt them, Kelly?"

"He killed them."

"Note the patient is fidgeting her thumbs." There was scribbling during the long, awkward silence. Dr. Brookside finally spoke again. *"Why did he kill them, Kelly?"*
"Because I told them about him."

"Okay. So, will he kill me too, then, if you tell me about him?"

"Yes. He will." Kelly's voice sounded firm at that answer.

"Well, I still would like to know about him. Can you please tell me just a little bit about him?"

"No, Doctah B... I can't tell you about him. I just can't."

"Are you afraid of him, Kelly?"

There was a pause. James could only hear the sound of more scribbling. There was a sound as if Dr. Brookside was picking up the recorder, and in a very hushed tone, he told the recorder, *"The subject's eyes are shut, but they are swelling up in tears."*

More scribbling sounds. The recorder was placed back down on the table. After another moment, Kelly finally replied, *"Yes. I am."*

"You are safe in this room, Kelly. Whatever we talk about stays between the two of us. No one will ever know."

"No." Kelly's voice was once again firm. *"He will find out. He always finds out."*

"How will he find out, Kelly?"

"All I can tell you is that he hides in the shadows."

"Okay. Well, can we talk about how you found your family dead, then?"

"Yeah. I can do that."

Another momentary pause. Then, she continued. *"I came home after spending time with my boyfriend, Duane. We been datin' for about six months now. We hung out at the karaoke bar that night, it was... I'd say... 'bout three in the morning when he dropped me off at home."*

"Okay, go on."

"I went into the backyard. I didn' want to wake up anyone in the house. There's an old white wooden lattice lookin' thing going up the side of the house, next to my bedroom window. ...That's on the second floor. Anyway, I left my window unlocked. I climbed up the lattice to my room an' slid opened the window to my room. I climbed into my room like I done many times. I'm so good at it now I don't make no noises. So, after climbing in my room... I walked to my door an' turned on the lights."

"Okay. When did you notice something was wrong?"

"The next day when I woke up. The house was oddly quiet."

"Okay, and how was the house being quiet odd?"

"Well, Doc, at my house in the mornings, things are far from quiet. My dad is usually downstairs fussin' about what is in the paper. My brother blares his music in the mornin' just to piss me off. Our dog chases our cat, Happy, an' my mom does the laundry."

"I see, now. I see. And then what happened?"

"Well, I went into my brother's room first."

"Okay. Did you notice anything strange in your brother's room?"

"No. My brother was at our family camp with our cousin, Heather, so his room was locked."

"So, your brother was not home, then."

"Yep, that's right. He wasn't home."

More scribbling by the Doctor. *"Then why did you try and go into his room?"*

"Well, my ma does the laundry in the mornin's, so, I checked to see if she was in his room. She was not."

"Because the door was locked."

"Right." A pause, more writing. The doctor never seemed to want to stop.

"Well, what did you do next, then?"

"I... I went to my parents' room next."

"Okay, Kelly. What did you find when you entered your parents' room?" There was about a minute of silence, save for the sound of the doctor's writing. The scribbling became faster as the silence went forth. James only wondered what the doctor could be looking at, or thinking, at that moment.

Finally, Kelly spoke again. *"I found my parents dead."* James could make out the girl quietly sobbing. *"Both of my parents... they were there, their bodies were cold and lifeless."*

"Can you tell me more details?"

"Yes, I... I can try. My dad was... lying face down on the carpet with a heavy, dark-colored blanket covering the lower half of his body."

"What about your mother?"

"She was propped up in their bed."

"Was her body also covered as well?"

"No. There were no covers on her."

"Can you try to describe to me how your mother looked?"

"I can try..." Kelly's voice became low, shallow with the tears of sadness. *"I can try, Doctah B."*

"It's okay, Kelly. Just take your time."

"Okay. My mom was wearing a blue lace nightgown. Her head was propped downward to the right side, her neck protruding upward, I want to say. There was a massive hole in the... in the back of her head. It took up most the back of her head, it did. The bed, along with her nightgown, was soaked in blood. Pieces of her brain were stuck to their white headboard. It..." A momentary pause. *"It... looked like pink and red chewed up gum, I'd say? The small chunks looked like ground-up pork, or maybe hamburger meat. As I got closer to my mother, I noticed she also had several very deep stab wounds around her waist. The bottom of her blue gown was shredded to pieces."*

"What about your dad, Kelly. Can you tell me more about him?"
"No. I ran out the room fast as I could."

"What did you do after you ran out of the room?"

"I ran into my room and then... that's when... HE came into my room."

"Was he already there inside your house?"

"Doctor Brookside, he is always with me." Her voice had suddenly changed; James could picture her curving her lips into a smile.

"What happened after he came into your room?"

"He looked at me with an evil grin on his face. He said to me, 'You see? You see now what happens when someone speaks of what they shall not speak of.'"

"Hmm. Interesting words. So, what did you do next after he told you that, Kelly?"

"Well. I ran downstairs quickly as I could, and I called the police."

"Thank you, Kelly. Please excuse me for one minute." James heard what sounded like Dr. Brookside placing his notebook and pen down onto the table. Then, it sounded as if water were pouring into a paper cup from a distance. *"Would you like some water, Kelly?"*

"No thanks, Doctor B."

Another momentary pause, and then the sound of Dr. Brookside picking up the tape recorder. After another minute, he began talking. *"I am beginning to wonder if what Kelly is telling me is the truth. Did it happen the way she told me, or is it a lie? I will have to press the subject further."*

The sound of footsteps walking to a location unknown, then, the cassette recorder was placed back onto the table. *"Okay, Kelly. Are you ready to continue our session?"*

"Yes, I am, Doctor B."

CHAPTER 10

James was still sitting on the cold, dirty floor in the room, listening to the recorded session. He raised the volume up on the tape player; he thought he might have heard some heavy breathing in the background.

"So, what happened after you called the police?" Dr. Brookside asked Kelly.

"I can't remember too much after that. All I can recall is what happen after the cops got there. They found me sittin' on my bed."

"Okay, so the cops are in your home and there in your room. Can you tell me what happened next?"

"It was weird. One minute, I was sitting down on the edge of my bed and the next... I was standing in the middle of the room. My hands were covered in blood."

"While the cops were still in your room?"

"Yes."

Dr. Brookside let out an audible, but low, sigh. *"Okay, so why were your hands covered in blood?"*

"I don't know." Kelly let out a soft whimper. James heard what sounded as if she was wiping her eyes with the back of her hand.

"But, I do remember looking down and... in my left hand. There was a large knife. The knife had a thick, red liquid dripping from the edge of the blade. As I looked around the bedroom... I saw him again."

Dr. Brookside clicked his pen open and closed several times, then placed it down. After a moment, James could hear the scribbling continue.

"Okay, Kelly. What was he doing?" he asked her.

"He was standing outside my bedroom window. He had that same grin on his face again... it creeps me out."

More pen on paper noise, and then, the Doctor asked, skeptically, *"He was standing outside your window?"*

"Yes, he was."

"How can that be? You told me your bedroom was on the second floor."

The audio ended abruptly. James quickly flipped the cassette over to try and hear the rest of the session, but the other side was blank; only dead static played. "Huh. Dr. Philip Brookside... now, why does that name sound so familiar?" James asked himself. "I can't think of where I've heard that name before. Oh well... time to head to the medical ward."

James stood up, placing the map and cassette player in his left pocket. The elasticity of the pants made it possible for James to hold both items in place. As James exited the room, he could feel his body become a lot weaker now than before due to blood loss. The desolate hallway now felt longer to James.

As he tried to make his way back to the stairway door, James could hear a faint whispering just a few yards off. The whisper sounded like a young lady's voice. The sound was subtle. "Help me, please help me."

"Hello? Is there anyone there?" James yelled as he slowly walked down the hall with the help of his cane. "Can you help me, please, sir?" The woman's voice continued to ask. "Hello. My name is James. Can you please tell me where you are? Maybe I can help you."

James stopped just a few feet from the door; he turned back to look where the cries of help were coming from. *They must be coming from inside one of the rooms.* James remembered that there were only three doors on this floor, along with the door to the stairwell.

Ok... so there is the main door that I can't open. There's the door to the room I was just in. The only door left is that other locked door. Maybe that's where the voice is coming from? James wondered. The voice again called out for help. This time, instead of a soft cry for help, the lady screamed in a blood-curdling pitch that rang through James' ears. He placed his hands around his ears trying to stop the ringing. It was then that he noticed what looked to be the silhouette of a woman on the ground. "Where is the shadow coming from?" he asked himself, still trying to protect his ears. Suddenly, a cold breeze shot past him.

James then saw the shadow on the checker title floor start to swing back and forth. He tilted his head back and looked up to see a young woman. She looked to be a nurse, dressed in an all-white uniform, hanging from a thick rope tied to one of the ceiling's two-by-four beams. Her neck looked clearly to be snapped in half. James looked on in horror as the nurse's limp body slowly started to turn toward him as it swung.

He could just barely make out her face; her semi-long light brown hair covered it. “I’m sorry,” James told as he lowered his head in respect. He closed his eyes for a second.

“Help me!” This time the voice sounded louder closer. James opened his eyes to look up once more, frightened at what he was seeing.

The corpse of the young nurse was starting to move. Her eyes opened. The dark, hollowed, empty eye sockets of the nurse locked onto James as she lowered her head down. He could see worms and maggots dart in and out from the hollowed-out eye sockets. As the nurse opened her mouth, a thick, black goo-like substance started to pour out from her mouth as if it were slow-moving black lava. She let out a shrill scream while dropping towards the floor in front of James. The rope jerked, suspending her fetid corpse just a couple of feet from the ground. Her lower teeth were a shining black whenever her mouth opened.

James began to back up slowly towards the stairway door. The nurse's body began to twist and move. The loud popping sound of broken bones echoed throughout the hallway as her right arm began to move up towards the rope. She grabbed the rope above her head with her rotten, decaying blue-gray hand. Dark blue veins pulsated. They ran down her arm as if they were dark ice water. She suddenly yanked hard on the rope, snapping it, and the nurse fell to the ground. James watched in horror; his eyes widened with a fixed gaze on the nurse as he continued to back up towards the door of the stairwell. The nurse slowly picked herself up onto her feet. She looked directly at James as she began walking towards him. James could hear the popping and clanking of her bones as she moved. Her matted, dusty hair and her decade of dried flesh of was nothing compared to the foul odor pouring forth from her body.

Suddenly, the undead nurse began to lunge at James, screaming a demonic yell. Her arms stretched out towards James with her fingers shaped in a claw-like pose. James' back suddenly plopped onto the door. He tried to grab the handle of the door but fumbled several times trying to open it. The nurse was getting closer and closer to him. James managed to quickly open to the entrance and fell backward onto the gray stairwell floor. He could still see the nurse racing towards him, her arms still stretched out her. Her hands widened as her fingers bent into a claw shape. The blood-curdling screams cut through the dead silence of the hallway like butter. The screaming terrified James; he quickly kicked the hatch hard with his left foot and it slammed shut with a loud thud. James rushed to lock the door just as the nurse was reaching it.

His back was now against the freezing iron opening. James dropped onto the ground, trying to wrap his head around what had just happened.

CHAPTER 11

"What... what the hell, that lady was dead, but she...?" James said in disbelief as he moved away from the door. Still on the ground, James backed away from the opening, his gaze ever fixed on the small window in the center of the locked door. His back slammed against the first step. He could still feel his heart beating fast, almost as if it were about to burst forth from his chest. "Maybe what I had just seen was my mind playing tricks on me. Yeah, that has to be it," James told himself, trying to rationalize what had just happened. He never did believe in ghosts; to him, they were always just an idle explanation to the unknown. He took a deep breath and cleared his head. As he got back up to his feet and walked to the door, he peered out of the window into the hallway. It was empty now; no signs of the nurse that was after him. It was as if nothing had happened at all. "I have to get out of this place," James said to himself.

As James made his way up the stairs, he began to feel more famished then before. "I need to find some food soon or I will pass out," James muttered to himself as he climbed towards the fifth floor. The horror of passing out inside this place, never to see his family again, scared him. The gritty, muddy steps were putting more and more strain upon his right leg. A constant stabbing pain shot through his leg with every step he took. Doubts about seeing his family again started to creep into his mind more and more. "I must not give up. I will see Liz and Amber again!" James told himself as he fought through the pain.

James finally made it onto the fifth floor. He opened the door and entered the eerie hallway. He closed the door behind him and took out the folded map from his pants pocket. He was glancing at the map as he used his cane to stand upright.

Okay, so, according to the map, If I am reading it right, then the medical ward is… just past the atrium walkway, the last door to the right. James peered down the nearly dark hallway as he folded the map up and tucked it back in alongside the cassette player.

He proceeded down the hall towards the atrium. A nervous chill washed over him like a blanket the closer he walked towards the dark voice before him. The fear of what might be waiting for him in the dark nearly froze him in place, but James knew that if he remained in that place then he would never see his family again. After what seemed like an eternity of walking, James finally came to the fork in the hallway. Two of the longer corridors had light, however, the illuminations down the passages were weak and dim. One was the hallway James had just emerged from; the other was the hallway to his left.

The corridor on the right was so dark, it appeared as if no light could ever hope to penetrate. "Down that corridor is where the medical room is at. Down that hallway is where I need to go," James sighed as he took a moment to look down the dread-filled empty void. James took a breath to mustered up his courage and then proceeded onwards.

As he walked closer and closer towards the darkness that resided there, James could almost hear laughter like that of a child coming from the deep abyss. Wobbling a bit, he made his way toward the left side wall for extra balance and support. Then with another deep breath, he pressed onward into the darkness that was now covering the hallway. The palms of his hands were beginning to sweat as fear began to grip him. James could now see the physical changes in the hallway taking place right before his eyes. Even though one half of the corridor was covered in darkness, the other half was not. The two different atmospheres swirled and mingled with one other. James noticed the edges of the floor disappearing into the emptiness.

"I don't know that this floor is safe to walk on," James said as he cautiously started to venture into the darkness. "I can't turn back now. I must get to the medical supplies." As he entered the darkness his vision became blinded with nothing. He could only rely on his hearing and his touch. James hugged the wall as he moved further into the black void. He soon heard a whistling sound echoing from deep as he pressed onward. The passageway felt colder than the others and heavier. James stopped in his tracks to get a better feel of the wall. He then realized that this hallway was once lined with windows. As he carefully ran his hand back and forth on the boarded-up window frames he could feel tiny shards of broken glass still attached.

James was trying to see if there was any wind coming into the building from outside. But they couldn't find anything; all the windows were sealed up tight with board-supported stone slabs. *If all the windows are now all sealed up, then why is this hallway so much colder than the others, and where did the noise I heard moments ago come from?* He made one more pass with his hand across the wall where the windows once were. He soon felt a sharp pain in his right hand as he cut himself on the edge of a sharp piece of glass. "Motherfucker!" James yelled in pain as he felt the burning of his skin splitting apart; warm blood was rushing down the palm of his right hand. He grabbed the bottom of his shirt and ripped it, then wrapped the torn cloth around his right hand trying to stop the bleeding. "Great. Now both my hands are wrapped up," James said as he pressed on deeper into the darkness. The more he walked down the corridor, the more it felt like he would never make it to the other side. James had an unnerving feeling as if he were being watched by something in the dark.

"Wh- who's there? I have a gu- gun." James said with a crackle in his voice. "I'll shoot you!"
He waited for someone, or something, to respond but nothing came forth. Only the eerie sound of the wind whistling through the hallway

could be heard, echoing loudly in the darkness. James kept on reminded himself about Amber and Liz; he would do anything to get out of this place to see them again.

To take is mind off of what was going on as he pressed on, James began to hum one of their favorite songs. It made James feel more relaxed and confident as he walked towards the atrium. He almost forgot that something was watching him. The tempo in his voice picked up with the music that he was humming. As the tempo began to lower, James felt a tug on his left pants leg. He stopped humming the song. "Hello?" he said as he leaned over to pass his hand around both legs. He tried to feel if something was still there. There was nothing there, just a feeling of emptiness lingering in the air. He was a bit relieved but growing very worried now. "Okay. I know I felt a tug on my pants. It felt just like Amber used to do when she was three." His heart was now beating a little bit faster and his forehead was beginning to bead up with sweat. He was now moving a bit faster out of a sudden fear creeping into his skin. "Am I almost near the end now?" he asked himself.

Just then, James heard three louder knocks coming from the hall behind him. "Hello?" James said nervously as he stopped dead in place. He was hoping that someone would answer. He felt as if maybe someone else was trapped in here other than himself. He took another breath and carried on ahead. After a few more steps, he heard the knocking again. This time, it was closer and louder than before. James didn't stop this time; he continued to move forward, hoping to reach the end soon. The knocking kept getting closer and closer, louder and louder. His mind was now racing. "What could be making those knocking sounds?" he mumbled to himself.

There was no visibility in the hallway to see what might be lurking there with him. James thought up a few possibilities of what could be making those knocking sounds. *It could be the wind moving through the pipes in the building; yeah, that's it. It just the wind in the old rusted pipes. These old buildings do have loose pipes that move and bang all the time.*

The knocking was now coming from both below and above him. Suddenly, the temperature in the building turned much hotter than before. The cold wind that once blew past him was no more. Instead, what was now passing across him was waves of heat and a soft-spoken, whispering voice. The voice only repeated the same words. "I see you. I see you. You will soon belong to me, little rabbit." The voice had an almost animal-like growl to it each time it spoke.

James moved as fast as he could. He felt as if something behind him was reaching out, trying to grab him. James knew he had to get out of the hallway fast. The cane skidded onto the floor, nearly causing James to fall as he tried to rush to the end of the hallway. He used the wall as a boost to help him move faster. The feeling was now stronger than before; James could now feel the iciness of long fingernails brush against the back of his neck. Finally, he made it out of the dark hallway. But James did not stop even then. He kept moving onward, not daring to look back. Within less than five minutes James finally came to the place that was on the map: two large glass doors that had the words *Medical Ward* etched into them.

CHAPTER 12

James was relieved a bit that the hallway had some light. "Okay, let's see now if there's still an active first aid kit somewhere in here that I can use." He began to rummage around the medical ward. The hallway was smaller than the ones he had previously walked down before. The medical ward itself was only about four and a half rooms combined.

James noticed that there were two doors on both sides of the passageway. "This has to be the smallest corridor I have ever seen," he said to himself out loud while walking. There was an old metal gurney outside one of the rooms. It was laced with rust spots along its' silverish railings, along with a dusty old white bed mattress laid loosely upon it. The mattress was old and in tatters. There was some stuffing hanging out from a torn, unstitched side of the mattress. James also noticed what looked to be a large, yellow stain in the middle. The wheels were not all present; two of them were missing.

James entered the tiny, nearly dark room next to the gurney. "Room 522A, Huh?" James said as he walked in. The walls were like those found within the rest of the building, an off-white color. From the archway, James peered into the bathroom to his right. Thanks to the lights in the hallway that illuminated the room just enough, James could see roaches crawling out the sink. A mirror that hung above it was broken. Several pieces hugged the edges of the frame while the rest laid scattered on top of the tile floors. James turned his head away from the bathroom entrance. There he saw an old wooden bed frame in the corner. James looked around the room for a bit and examined the small nightstand as well as the large dresser near the bed. Both were empty. He came across a white metal box on the wall.

First Aid Kit, the box claimed in large red lettering. "Yes!" James exclaimed, relieved as he walked towards it. He was trying to hide the pain in his leg, but it felt incredibly overwhelming. He was now in more pain than ever before. His right leg was now the mixed color of an onyx and amethyst shard. The back of his head was faring no better. He grabbed the metal box and, as he tried to open the box, it fell off the wall. The screws that had the first aid kit bolted to the wall broke. James set the box down onto the nightstand and opened it. To his dismay, the box proved to be empty. Nothing was inside of it, not even a wrapper to a single Band-Aid.

James made his way out of the room and went into 521B. It was directly across from the room he was just inside. "I need to find something to help me bandage up my wounds fast," James said to himself. As he walked into the room, James' eyes darted from left to right, right to left as he quickly scanned the area.
This place was in the same condition as the previous room. The only difference was the small, green vase sitting in the middle of the nightstand. There were wilted flowers in the emerald vase that drooped over the edge. James walked up to the wall and grabbed the first aid kit. It, too, broke off the wall. He placed the first aid kit onto the bed and opened it. Empty. As James continued to search each room in the medical wing, he began to feel nervous at the thought that there might not be any medical supplies left in the hospital. Terror crept into James' mind that the last breath he would ever take might be inside this abandoned hospital. With doubt now racing in his head, James pressed on with the hope that he would soon be seeing his family again. As James came to the second to last door in the hallway, he found it to be open. James walked into the room. This room was different from the previous rooms he had just come from; instead of a bed, there was a small cot located against the far wall. There was no vase on the nightstand; sitting upon it was an old brass picture frame with an old faded photograph.

The picture was that of a middle-aged woman and a little boy. She was wearing what looked to be an old 1930's style white cream dress. Her hair was neatly pulled back and she appeared to be in her late forties. The boy wore long pants and a long-sleeve button-up shirt, appearing to be about thirteen years old. James picked the frame up as on the bottom of the picture he could see some writing. The note read, "Look to me to be your guide." Confused a bit on what this saying could mean, he continued to stare at the picture for clues.

James sat down on the bed and inspected the frame. The brass plating upon it was held together by two pieces on the back. James turned the frame over, undid the tabs, and quickly removed the picture from its' dwelling. On the back of the picture was another small, hand-drawn map of the hospital. This map was different than the one he had previously found before. There were three areas circled on this copy. Each had a symbol of a key located next to them. James took the photo, folded it in two, and placed it with the other map he already possessed. He then continued the search for the first aid kit but still could find nothing. "There has to be something still left in here that I can use," James said as he went back to search the area one more time. As James walked out of the last room, the makeshift cane cradled under his right hand, his face retained a disappointed and frustrated look upon it. His eyebrows sloped inward. Searching the area, he came across a brown door labeled *Medical Supplies Closet. 522B.* James twisted the knob and the door creaked open with ease.

The room was no bigger than the walk-in closet in his home's master bedroom. There were only eight shelves total, all painted white. Both sides had four shelves screwed into the wall. In the back of the room were several hooks screwed into the back wall. Hanging on a few hooks in the back was a set of first aid kits. Each shelf had been labeled by the type of supplies contained upon them.

James couldn't read the labels due to the dim lighting of the building. He made his way towards the back wall and grabbed one of the first aid kits from its hook hoping that there would still be something left inside. He placed it on the nearest empty shelf and opened it.

Inside the box was a roll of gauze and a several high-grade Band-Aids. James quickly grabbed the items. He also found a bottle that read Pentazocine. As James read the label, he figured out this was a type of anabolic steroid doctors used to treat moderate to severe pain. James looked inside the old red and white hard plastic container for a syringe, but he could not find one. He checked the other three kits on the wall. They were all empty. James then started to dig through every shelf and drawer in the room. After several minutes of searching, he came across an unopened plastic bag. He grabbed the bag with haste and sat down on the dirty floor of the supply closet. He sat close to the door to try getting as much light as he could to see. He carefully took a syringe out of the sealed bag, unscrewed the cap, and placed the needle into the thick white plastic lid of the bottle. Not knowing how much or if any medicine was still left in the bottle James flipped it upside down and proceeded to draw out, to his amazement, a full vial of the liquid medication. He then placed it on the ground and rolled up his right pant leg.

He could not see how much worse his leg had become. James jabbed the needle into his leg. "AHHH MOTHERFUCKER!" he yelled as he injected half of the syringe contents into his right leg. James could feel the fiery sting of the medicine as it was coursing through his veins. After he placed the syringe back upon the floor, he took the gauze out the box, unrolled it and began to tightly wrap his leg. The pain was overwhelming. James then realized how bad of a condition his leg was in. He could feel the pain shooting through his entire body as he continued to tightly wrap his leg. After what seemed like forever, James was finished applying the wrapping.

He sealed the gauze around his leg with a few of the heavy-duty metal hooked Band-Aids he had found. Wrapped as it was, his leg was twice as large as it had been. James then began to wrap bandaging tightly around his arm. He was hurting severely from the pain. James tapped his right forearm several times, hard. As he continued to tap the upon the same spot, he could see his vain starting to appear. He picked up the syringe, now half-filled with the steroid, from the ground and injected the liquid into his arm. He hoped that the liquid would give him some type of relief even for a moment. Just like before, a blazing fire shot up his arm.

As he sat on the floor and relaxed, he pulled out the photo of the old woman and young boy. James studied the map on the back. There was one room close to him that was not circled but possessed a very dark, penciled-in Triangle. “I don’t know why but I feel I have to check out that room before I leave here,” James told himself.

CHAPTER 13

James eagerly jumped back to his feet and tucked the picture away, leaving the room. He proceeded down the hall towards the room marked on the photograph's map. *Man, this place is depressing,* James thought as he headed towards it. A moment later he finally reached the door. "What? What happened here?" James said as he looked at part of the broken door lying on the floor in the hallway. The other part of the door was barely hanging on the bent frame by a single copper hinge. The old painted white door was broken in half. The bottom part of it appeared to have been kicked hard from the inside. The broken and exposed splinters of wood were curved outward facing the hallway. The wooden frame was bent in such a way that the rest of the door had no hope of ever closing properly again. James could see termites eating away at the delicious rot. There were no signs of numbers etched upon its' surface.

When James walked into the room he could sense this place was different than the others. This area felt much colder than any other he had visited so far. The lights from the hallway barely illuminated the darkness inside. The dim glow was just bright enough for James to notice there were no shelves on the wall, no file cabinets, no desk anywhere to be found. The room was laid completely bare. The only thing that suggests this place once held anything in it was a weird dark stain in the middle of the floor.

James pulled the photo out to look at the map. "This is the place, right? This is the room marked; surely it has to be it," James said to himself, uncertain. He peered around the room now, more confused as to why this area was marked on the map and why it was empty. He began to come up with some theories of what might have happened here.

"Well, there's no point in checking the room anymore. I won't find anything useful here," he said to himself. James started to walk out into the hallway when his eyes caught a small glimpse of what looked to be a secondary shadow of upon the wall. He turned around to see if anyone else was nearby. Then, he turned his head to look back at the wall. The second shadow was still there. Thinking that it still belonged to him, James raised his right arm towards the ceiling. The shadow on the wall also raised its' right arm, as well as the shadow on the ground. James then raised his left arm and simultaneously both shadows did the same. Satisfied that both entities belonged to him, James proceeded out of the room. As he exited the room the wall shadow was still there. A sinister smile appeared across its' face as its' right hand began to wave at James.

James decided to check out the other three marked places that were on the map. *Okay, so, the nearest mark on the map is on the fourth floor. I will head there next. Hopefully, I will be able to find something I can use,* thought James as he exited the medical ward and entered the main hallway. He spotted several rats scurrying on the ground as he looked down the hallway at the dark void. That old feeling of dread once again waved over James as the hair on the back of his neck stood up. James turned and walked down the other end of the hallway. After a few minutes of walking the corridor, James come across the doorway to the stairwell as well as an elevator. He paused for a moment and took a deep breath. "Man, I wish those damned elevators worked. But then again, the way this place is, the cable would most like snap and I'd be falling to my death," he said as he placed his hand on the handle and opened the door to the stairway.

A loud ding echoed throughout the hallway. James turned his head over towards the elevator. Just then the two metal doors slid open and a tall, very thin, pale man wearing black four-button suit stepped out of the elevator. James watched, too paralyzed with fear to walk away. The apparition did not attempt to even look at James; instead, he made his way down the hall. James watched as the mysterious figure disappeared into the dark void. A few seconds later James snapped himself out of his trance. As he grabbed the door handle again the thin man appeared behind him.

"Run, little rabbit, RUN!"

James could feel the sinister smile man as he finished his words. He grabbed the handle and swung the door to the stairs open. Without thinking about his hurt leg James rushed down the stairs.

While climbing down the stairs James couldn't shake the feeling that he was still being followed. Once he made it to the fourth floor, his stomach began to growl with pain. "It's been a while since I last had anything to eat," he complained out loud as his stomach bellowed and ached. The fact that he had forgotten what or when his last meal came scared him. Food, however, was the last thing on his mind.

James reached the entrance to the fourth floor and opened it. He then took out the map, which he placed in between the elastic band his pants and his hip. "Okay, according to the map the room I'm looking for is *410*; it's the third door down on the right," James muttered to himself, putting the map back into his pants. The floors and rooms were all starting to look the same to him now. It was getting harder and harder for him to tell what floor he was on and the difference between each room as well.

James finally found the room and walked in. The room contained several wooden desks. They were all spread out a few feet apart from one another. There was two large metal cabinet on the back wall. There were remnants of what looked be a widow frame. The slight hint of a border was still there but the windows were all bricked up. The room contained just one chair; the others seemed to be missing. As usual, only the lights from the hallway provided any illumination.

James quickly began to check the desk to his right. There was a small but rectangular dark green case on the far right side of it. This box had some designs carved into it, but it was far too dim to truly make out what the markings were. James did find on its' surface a small lock. He dug around the desk to see if there was anything in the drawers that he could use to pick the lock, but he found nothing except for some old paperwork. James abandoned this desk and headed to inspect the one next to it, but that desk, too, was empty. He did not bother checking the one located in the middle of the room; James had an uneasy feeling wash over him when he simply looked at it. *I'll leave this one for last.*

James then began searching through the file cabinets. As he looked through each of the drawers the tracks would squeak as the stiff plastic rollers slid back and forth. James found some files and folders in the second cabinet as well as an old burlap sack, its' light tan having faded with time. The leather was dry and cracking. He took this dusty handbag out of the draw, patting it several times to make sure nothing was living inside it. Each hit on the leather caused dust to fly into the air. James coughed as the dust entered his lungs. He then opened the top flap of the bag to see if anything remained inside but it was empty. *I can still use it, though,* James figured as he removed the contents of his pants and loaded them into the bag. He then draped the handbag around his shoulder and fastened the strap before he continued to search the room more items.

In another file cabinet, James came across a brown notebook. Picking it up and wiping the thick dust from its' cover he headed for the doorway. Using the meager light, James opened the notebook only to be greeted with a cloud of dust. After clearing the dust from his vision, he began to flip through its' contents. The pages had turned a dark yellow and became brittle over the years. Only the first few pages had writing on them; the rest were left blank. James could feel his right leg begin to give out once more. He didn't have the strength to hold himself up even with his cane. He walked to the nearest chair in the room, rolled the chair toward the desk closest to the door, and sat the notebook onto its' surface. James began to read.

Dec. 23. 1986

Hello, my name is Ashley Moore. I am a nurse here at St. Mary's Hospital. Over the last few months, I have noticed that Dr. Coffin began acting very strangely. He would ask to have one or more of our mental patients be moved from the east wing to the upper part of the north wing. We would see the patients maybe one or two more times after they were moved... then, never again. All records of the patients would mysteriously vanish as if that patient had never been here at St. Mary's to begin with. After a few months of this, one day I decided to follow Doctor Coffin as he went down to the basement of the hospital. I hid behind a concrete pillar next to the stairs. Doctor Coffin was there with two other staff members and one of the patients. The three of them were wearing dark robes; they were of the kind you would find worn by the clergy of an old church. The patient was wearing just his regular gray pants and strapped to a gurney. The straps were fastened across his chest, head, arms, and legs. The basement was cold and dark. I might not have seen anything if it wasn't for the six lit candles that were fixed to the basement's stone walls.

The two staff members were chatting in an unknown language as Doctor Coffin took out a large, curved knife. The knife featured an engraving of goat's head on its' handle. Doctor Coffin started cutting the patient repeatedly. First, his throat, then his right wrist, then his left. The patient must have been heavily drugged because he didn't scream for help or attempt to get free. I watched in horror as massive amounts of blood ran out of his body, twitching compulsively on the gurney in shock. The blood ran off the gurney into three clay bowls. They then took the blood-filled bowls and drew up a six-star pentagram on the four corners of the wall. I ran upstairs; I couldn't handle witnessing anything more. It's been three months now and I'm fearing for my life. I feel like I'm being constantly watched as if I might be the next one to be going missing. Today is Friday, the 23rd of December. As I walked into work, I noticed that Doctor Coffin had put in a new metal security door on the main entrance. He told our staff it will help prevent the patients from escaping. The door can only be opened by three key cards and an eight-digit numeric code. Before he left to go to his office, he asked me if I would like to move to the north wing. I told him that I would think about it. I'm afraid that I may not have too much longer to live. I wrote down the eight digital numeric code for the door. I wrote the pieces of the code on four separate sheets of paper, hiding them in various locations of this hospital.

One is on the back of an old photograph of my dad when he was a kid and my grandmother. I drew a map of where I placed the torn papers with the codes written on them. I believe the key cards are the name badges of the three doctors that run this hospital. I must find a way to get out of this place before I end up like the rest. I will try to collect the name badges tonight on my shift. I just hope-

The writing in the notebook ended abruptly. James flipped through it trying to find if anything else of value but most of the remaining pages had been torn out.

“So, I need to find the four torn pages in this hospital maze. Each page has part of the eight-digit code that the nurse wrote down. Ok… doesn’t sound too hard.” James said to himself, trying to sound optimistic. As he was placing the notebook on the desk, James spotted a small, shiny pin poking out the back cover. He opened the back of the book to reveal a ripped page pinned onto the back of the notebook. He removed and unfolded the paper to see three numbers. James could barely make out the numbers because of how faded they were with time. However, there was just enough ink present to make out *8-2-7.*

CHAPTER 14

James hastily searched the drawers for a pen or a pencil to write with. He managed to find a small shard of a pencil buried deep in the back of the middle drawer. It had no eraser on it and bared teeth marks on the wood, but James didn't care. He opened the notebook and ripped a blank page out, placing the torn sheet on the desk. Onto this paper, James copied down the numbers *8-2-7* in bold print. He wondered why the nurse hadn't just put all eight numbers on multiple sheets of paper and hid them all over the hospital. The bigger question, however, concerned Doctor Coffin and what had truly happened down in the basement. After a few moments, James took a deep breath and stood up. "Okay, now it's time to go try and look for the rest of those numbers, as well as the three badges so I can get hell out of here and see my family again," James said to himself as he put the notebook and paper with the three numbers in the bag and headed out into the hallway.

It feels like I've been stuck in this place for several days now, and yet, it's still nighttime, James thought to himself as he rubbed his right thumb and index finger back and forth across his chin. James could feel tiny, pointed hairs prick him. "What? I have hair on my chin? That can't be right. I shaved before I left for work today. How long have I been trapped in here?" His mind was racing. Every morning before work, James would get up, brush his teeth, and shave. Liz thought his smooth face made him look sexy. He tried growing a beard but there were just too many patches and Liz hated the way it looked on him. "It takes me at least a few days without shaving to get my facial hair to grow this long..." He told himself while walking down the hall. The pain in his right leg was coming back as the medicine started to wear off.

Hungry, weak and tired, James' only drive now was his determination to see his wife and daughter again. He thought on several occasions that he had heard their voices echoing in the hallways. He knew that couldn't be since he was the only person trapped in this place. James stopped for a second to gain his composure as tears fell from his face. Realizing how badly he wants to be with his family, whispers of faint memories with his wife and daughter echoed throughout his head. James was now more determined to find the Items scattered throughout the hospital so he can go home.

The long, dark hallway felt more and more intimidating as the hours passed by. There was a kind of eeriness to this old hospital. The dead quiet made the hospital feel bigger; In some ways, it even felt as if it were alive. James stopped and pulled out the map, looking to see where the next closest mark was to him. "Okay, so, the next closest mark on the map is this room at the end of the hallway," he told himself as he placed his finger atop the white line on the map and followed it to the room. James picked up the map and made his way to room *413*. As James opened the door, an uneasiness crept upon him.

CHAPTER 15

This room was markedly different from the other rooms James had visited on this floor. The dim hallway light barely reached past the first couple of feet in the room. It was just enough light for James to see that the walls were covered in white and dark blue ceramic tiles, the same type as you would find in a public bathroom. The floor was made of plain concrete and featured several bathtubs spread out into rows. James walked towards one of the tubs to see what, if anything, was in there. The lack of light made it difficult for him to see.

The hall light was able to reach the first few bathtubs, but barely. The tub was an old 1950's porcelain type, white with four tiny curved legs bolting it to the floor. Rust stain patterns covered the entire tub. James knelt next to the tub and put pressed his hand onto the cold, porcelain bottom of the tub; it was empty. "Nothing in here," James said as his right hand swept the bottom of the tub. His fingers glided across the smooth surface. After a few minutes of checking, James got back to his feet. *Man, I can only imagine what kind of horrors were going through the patients' minds. They must have been forced to take baths together in this room. That must have been humiliating for them. I could never.* James was all at once sympathetic to the plight of these people he had never met, trying to imagine what it would have been like.

As he continued to search for the second torn page in the dark, a small noise echoed loudly throughout the room. It sounded like a sink or faucet dripping water at a slow pace. At first, the sound didn't bother James as his mind was focused on nothing but the torn page he was looking for. But as time went on, the constant sound of the water dripping slowly began to get the best of him.

Drip... drip... drip... drip... drip... drip... The water splashing on the ground was now echoing louder throughout the room. James closed his eyes to try blocking the noise from his mind, but it was like a phantom itch on his back that he just couldn't get rid of. He decided to find out where the dripping sound was coming from and turn it off. He checked the wall at the back of the room; nothing. Then he checked the left and right walls. He passed his hands up and down in a sweeping motion along the walls and still, he didn't find the source of the noise.

Drip... drip... drip... drip... drip... drip... The sound was echoing louder in the room, driving James more and more insane. He then started to search all of the tubs. One by one, James ran his hands along the cold, hard porcelain bottoms of every tub in the room. He was frantically checking for a plug or knob to pull. He was thinking maybe that there was some water still trapped in the closed faucets.
"If I can turn on the water and drain the tub, maybe the noise will go away," James said. But none the tubs had any knobs to turn on the water. "Wait, how do they... No, this can't be right. No knobs in the tub?" James said to himself, confused. The noise was getting so loud that his head was now starting to hurt with the pain of a migraine.

Drip... drip... drip... drip... drip... drip... "Where is that God damned dripping sound coming from?!" James shouted now in anger as he heard what sounded like a loud splash coming from one of the tubs near the back wall.

James snapped his gaze toward the back wall. "Hello? is anyone there?" he called out, trying not to sound as if fear were about to cripple his voice. He just stood in place, eyes frozen towards the back wall, waiting for someone, anyone, anything to walk out of the darkness towards him. The room was suddenly quiet now; no sound of dripping water nor that of another splash.

There was a faint sound of a rat squeaking near the doorway, but this didn't affect James, as his focus was shifted toward the darkness. "Hello? My name is James... is there anyone in the back there?" he asked, nervously. "I heard a splash... hello?"

After waiting for several minutes for an answer of any kind, James decided to continue searching the room for any clues. He thought to himself that maybe he just imagined the loud splash. As he was searching the room once more, within his peripheral vision James thought he had seen a dark figure standing in the doorway. The figure was tall and slinky. James walked to the door and peered out into the hallway but there was nobody there. I must be losing my mind, he wondered. *First, I'm hearing noises as if something is about to jump out of the tub; now I'm seeing dark figures. Get it together, man, get it together. I'm getting nowhere fast.*

James took a deep breath and pulled out the map. He walked into the doorway so that he could examine it once more to make sure this was the right room. As he was reading the map James felt something reach out and try to grab his left arm from within the dark. He quickly turned to look to see what it was but there was nothing there. "What the hell was that?" he asked himself as he looked back toward the map. "This is the room. But where is that page?"

He went back into the room one more time, determined to find his clue. He searched the entire room all over again. Once more the dripping sound echoed louder and louder throughout the room, making it harder for James to focus on finding the paper.

"Damn it, I wish that fucking noise would stop so I can concentrate. The map said it was in this room, but where is it?" James' head was pounding more and more now. "Is that torn page even in this fucking room?" James asked himself.

He slumped over onto the nearest tub and decided to take a small nap to get rid of his headache. *Maybe a good nap will help me think where it could be located,* he told himself as he slowly dropped his body onto the floor. *I'm just going to just... rest for a few minutes.* James closed his eyes.

CHAPTER 16

“Daddy, get up Daddy, Daddy, wake up.” A small voice cried in the darkness. James slowly wakes up, rubbing the sleep from his eyes to see his daughter Amber pulling his hand and shouting at him.

“Daddy, come on, we are going to miss it.”

“Miss what, Amber?” He asked his daughter, still trying to focus his blurry sight.

“The school fair is today. Get up, dad, or we’re going to miss the school fair today.”

“Okay, okay, slow down little one… let me get dressed quickly and then we will go. Make sure you’re ready in a few minutes.” James sat up on the edge of the bed.

Amber ran out of the room. James cleared the last remaining sleet from his eyes. “Why am I up this early on a Saturday?” He said in a groggy voice. “Because you promised your daughter if she did well in school you will take her to the fair.” Liz was standing at the sink in the master bathroom, running the water as she brushed her teeth.

“Why can't you go instead, Liz?” James replied while struggling to get dressed.

“Because I have work today,” Liz told James as she playfully threw a towel at him. James, half-dressed now, grabbed his wife by her left hand and pulled her in for a kiss.

"You need to get ready; your daughter is waiting for you downstairs," she said, pulling away. She stood before her husband was in a stage of half-dress.

James was in the bathroom now, brushing his teeth. He asked his wife, "So, why are you going in on a Saturday?"

"Mary is still out sick, so, Tanya asked if I could work today."

"Okay," James replied. Warm water was flowing out the faucet; it was time for the morning shave. After about thirty minutes, he was finally ready to leave. Amber was in her room listing to music, already dressed. Her iPod was playing a mix of songs from a few rock bands: Shinedown, Korn, Slipknot, and Disturbed.

Amber had heard her best friend Stephanie's older brother Austin play these songs in his room last time she slept over at their house. She had grown to like them ever since. James came downstairs wearing dark blue jeans and a blue collared shirt. "Bye, hun," he shouted. "Bye, mom, see you after the fair!" Amber also yelled as she raced down the stairs after her dad. She was wearing dark jeans with ripped holes in the knees and a black shirt that read *My Rules My World.* The two exited the house and got into James' car. Turning the ignition, roaring it to life, James asked his daughter, "Ready, Amber?" They took off for her school, only a fifteen-minute drive away.

As they walked toward Amber's school, James casually started to look around the area. He was seeing a lot of parents walking around with their kids. All of them seemed incredibly happy; maybe it because they don't have to wear their uniforms today, he thought. Everyone was eager for the fair as they all headed outside to the school's back yard. James looked at Amber as she called after him.

"Daddy, come on!" she squealed as she chased after some of her friends. "Coming, sweetheart," James called back to her as he followed behind the other parents.

As he walked outside with the other parents James saw how large the fair was. *There must be at least twenty-five booths here,* James thought as he watched the kids run-up to the booths like wild, hungry dogs. There were food and game booth as well as tables for the children to get their faces painted. James stood in the grass watching what all the other kids were doing. He became so fixated on the face painting station that he momentarily did not realize his daughter was tugging on his hand. "Daddy, Daddy!" shouted Amber in his ear.

"Yes, my love, what is it?" James mumbled, momentarily escaping from his trance. "Dad, can I have some money for the games?" she asked, sporting an eager look on her face.

"Alright, love, I will give you five dollars to go play, okay?"

"Thanks, Daddy, you're the best!" Amber told him as she gave her dad a big hug, swiping the Lincoln portrait from his hand as quickly as he pulled it out from his wallet. James watched as his daughter ran off to meet up with her friends. She was seven and a half years old now, growing more beautiful by the day.

"This is such a nice day," thought James as the warmth of the sun shined down upon him. The laughter of kids and the noisy but welcoming conversation of the other adults were entertainment to his ears. James walked up to a booth selling canned soft drinks. "Hello, sir, and welcome to St. Mary's 45th annual school fundraiser Fair," the gentleman behind the booth said. James paused for a moment. *Wait, what did he just say? Did he just say St. Mary's?* A nervous, panicked look crossed James' face.

"Sir, sir, excuse me, sir? Are you okay?" the man asked James.

"Oh... Oh, yeah, I'm fine. I just misheard what you said."

"Sir, I asked you if you wanted something to drink," the man told him. There was a line beginning to form now, and the man looked eager to move James along.

"Oh, yeah, a drink, yes. Yes, I'd like two drinks, in fact." James told him.

"Okay, sir, just pick two cans from the ice chest." James looked in the ice chest and grabbed two Dr. Peppers. This was his and Amber's favorite drink. "Here, I'll take these."

"Okay, good choice," said the man with a smile. "That will be two dollars."

James grabbed a pair of dollar bills from his wallet and handed them to the man, then walked off to look for his daughter. As he wandered the playground looking for Amber, he spotted a group of kids dashing between two booths. "Hey, they have some games over here, too!" one of the kids shouted towards one of his friends. James then turned his head and spotted his daughter at one of the face painting tables. Amber was with a group of her friends, and she was receiving a temporary face tattoo. James stood there for a bit to watch his daughter have fun. *Man, she will be eight in just a couple of weeks. I can't believe how time is just flying by.* He took a sip of his soft drink.

"Hey, dad," Amber said very happily as she walked up to him.

"Hey, little one, how are you enjoying the festival?"

"Oh, it's great dad. Me, Megan, Stephanie, and Bella all got matching tattoos."

"Tattoos!" James mocked surprise. "Are they real?" he asked with a sly grin across his face.

"Dad, you know that I'm too young for a real one!" she said sarcastically.

"Okay, okay, I was just asking." He pulled out the unopened Dr. Pepper. "Oh, hey love, I got you this."

"My favorite!" Amber said excitedly as her eyes grew wide with joy. "Thanks, Daddy, I love you so much!" She popped open the tab and began drinking the soft drink.

"Hey, I have a great idea. How about we go play a few games together, just you and me."

"Okay, dad, that sounds fun." She was trying to gulp down her drink as quickly as she could. "I know the first game I want to play."

"Okay, and what game is that?" James asked her.

"It's the ring toss game." Amber was tipping the can upside-down, trying to get the last drop to fall out.

"Okay, then, let's go toss some rings." As they walked toward the ring toss booth, Amber was rattling off a list of all the other games she wanted to play with her dad.

The school fair was running wild with kids hyped up on sugar, running from booth to booth to play the games, or to get food. The teachers and parents were trying their hardest to keep up with them. James and Amber made it to the ring toss line. The line was the average length for a school fair game. There were four kids in front of them. Amber spotted one of her friends, Aaron, who was walking past them while eating a slice of cheese pizza. "Hey, Aaron!" Amber yelled at him as she waved. Aaron looked at her and waved back, holding the half-eaten slice of pizza in his hand. "Hey, Dad, can we go get pizza after?" she asked.

"Hmmm, pizza, that does sound rather good. Yes, we can get some pizza after the game." James said.

After a few minutes of waiting it was finally Amber's turn. As she stepped up to the line to play the game, one of Amber's teachers, Ms. Lee, walked up to James. "Hey, Mr. Callaway, how are you doing today?" she asked James.

"Hi. I'm doing fine, just enjoying the fair with Amber," James replied with a smile. "I'm so sorry... I've forgotten your name."

"I am Ms. Lee, I'm Amber's biology teacher."

"Oh, Ms. Lee, forgive me, work has been nuts these past few weeks." James shook her hand. "How are you?"

"Oh, I'm doing fine," Ms. Lee replied. "I am glad I ran into you, though."

"Uh-oh," James said. It sounded like a mixture of joking and worried. "Oh, don't be worried about it. It's nothing bad, Mr. Callaway. It's about your daughter's grades in my class."

Okay, what's wrong with her grades? James silently thought. "I and her other teachers have discussed the fact that Amber may be eligible to take some high school courses. Her grades are phenomenal, and we feel that she is not getting challenged enough at the current level she is at."

"Wow! Um, okay. Wow." James said, shocked but proud. "Let me sit down with my wife and Amber and talk about maybe letting her take a few advance classes."

Ms. Lee smiled. Before walking away she told James, "Okay, well, let me know what you three decide."

"Daddy, Daddy, I won, I won!" Amber was full of glee as she held up a big pink stuffed bunny.

"That's great, my love," James replied.

"Oh, was that Ms. Lee, my teacher?"

"Yeah, we were just talking for a few minutes while you were playing."

"Oh, okay," Amber said. "She is the prettiest teacher in this school. Her blonde hair is always curly and she has the best green eyes." Amber was playing with her new stuffed animal. "So Daddy, can we go get some pizza now? I am so hungry."

James looked at his watch. 1:10pm. "Yeah, let's go get some pizza. I'm hungry, too." They both walked over to the pizza booth and waited in line.

"Hello, two slices of pizza, please, both cheese," James told the lady behind the counter once it was their turn to order. The worker handed James two paper boats each with a slice of cheese pizza. "Six dollars please." James paid while Amber found a bench for them to sit down and eat. As they sat and ate the hot pizza, gooey cheese dripped all over the bench as Amber began to eat. James could feel the warm crust and the hot cheese on his tongue as it melted in his mouth. "MMM, this is good!" Amber said with a big smile as she finished her slice. After they ate, both James and Amber went a purchased two more cans of Dr. Pepper to share. They were enjoying their time at the Fair.

Amber turned to her Dad. "Daddy, Daddy I found a torn page." James dropped the half-empty can of Dr. Pepper on the grass. Amber's words then became more and more like a faint echo as it was the only words James now hears on repeat in his head.
"I found a torn page. The torn page, Daddy." The noise of the Fair was fading as if James' ears had been submerged. Soon, it was muted completely, as if someone had pressed a button to turn off a TV. He could see the lips of kids and adults move as their mouths opened and closed but he could not hear any of the words. James watched as his daughter spoke to him but he couldn't hear anything she was saying. "The torn page" just kept echoing louder and louder in his head.

CHAPTER 17

James bolted up from his nap, shaken. "The torn page!" he shouted, breathing heavily. He sat on the floor looking around the room. James realized that the room was too dark for him to find the page he needed. "I will have to find a flashlight or a match and come back here," he murmured as he grabbed his makeshift cane. As he headed toward the door, he thought he had seen what looked like a figure of someone standing in the far left back corner of the room. James rubbed his eyes and looked again. This time, when his eyes became refocused, nobody was standing there. James proceeded to the doorway, thinking that the lack of blood, food, and sleep is causing his mind to play tricks on him. This damned place was making him see things that were not there.

James ventured out into the hallway once more and glanced down both pathways. After a brief hesitation, he decided to head back to the stairs. *Maybe I can find a flashlight in one of the upstairs rooms, or at least, one of the three badges,* he told himself as he passed a roach scurrying along the edge of a boarded window. While he walked, he could not help but feel uneasy. It was as if someone was once again following him. The hairs were standing up on the back of his neck and the dreaded feeling of someone staring him down had James on edge. Numerous times he would turn to look behind him to see if anyone there. Every single time he did, he just saw the same thing; a long, empty, poorly lit hallway filled with rats, roached, and their carcasses. The dim lights continued to sway as if vexed by an unseen wind. James could hear the buzzing of the faded lights trying with all their might to remain lit.

James began to approach the stairway door when he heard a loud thumping sound behind him. The noise repeated three times; it reminded James of a horses' hooves stomping on the ground. *Thump... thump... thump...* James' eyes grew wide with fear as sweat began trickling down his forehead. *There is nothing behind you. It's only your imagination playing tricks on you. You're the only one here,* James continued to reassure as he hastened towards the door. The heavy thumps were getting louder as they got closer to James. The ground shook with each thunderous crash. He could feel the heavy presence of something huge getting closer to him, almost as if they were on top of him. He opened the door and made his way up the stairs as quickly as he could, ignoring the pain in his leg and not once looking back or caring if the noise had stopped. James hurried up the stairs to the fifth floor.

When James reached the top of the stairway, he swung open the door. He walked a few feet before he stopped and looked at the map. There wasn't a circle marking on this floor. *Okay, well, I guess I'll see if I can find a flashlight in one of the rooms up here, at least.* He put the map away and continued charting a course down the hallway. While walking down this passage, James' head began to throb once more.

He began wiping off fresh blood that was running down the back of his head. Startled a bit, James struggled to remember how his wound got reopened but couldn't. *I must get out of this place and seek professional medical help,* he thought. As he passed up the first room he wondered what had made those stomping noises behind him on the fourth floor. It was at that moment that the speaker system sprang back to life. "Are we having fun yet, James?" a voice asked him. James stopped in confusion, wondering if this was another trick his mind was trying to play on him.

"You let me rot in jail because you were a shitty lawyer. Do you remember me, James? Because I remember you very well." The voice screeched over the aged P.A. system. James recognized the males' voice; he just couldn't put a name or a face to it. "So, since you left me to rot and never see my family again, I'm going to return the favor. I wonder how Liz is coping with you being gone for all this time. I bet Amber would need a new father figure now that
you're out of the picture. What do you say, James? Do you think I can be her new Daddy?"

"Don't you fucking dare go near them, you fucking asshole!" James momentarily forgot about his pain as he began to rage at the voice.

The putrid odor of rotten eggs, spoiled milk, and decaying skunk began to fill the hallway; James began coughing uncontrollably. His eyes began to water from the smell assaulting his senses. *I have to find someplace safe,* James thought to himself as he continued his hacking. The smell was becoming more and more unbearable. It offended greatly the back of his nose and throat like tiny, fiery needles. "Fuck, it smells like rotten piss," James exclaimed as he tried to cover his face with his shirt. "Who the hell are you!" James demanded in a raspy voice.

There was no response from the P.A. system. No buzzing or crackling noise; the speakers returned to their inactive state. James was feeling weak; his eyes were going in and out of focus as his head felt foggy. The smell was affecting him pretty hard.

He was about to pass out in the middle of the hallway when he finally reached a door to another room. *Okay, I'll start with this room and see if I can find a flashlight or lighter.* His coughing continued as he tried to cover his face. *I will save the first room I passed for last since I don't really feel comfortable near it.*

The next room he did reach was dusty, cluttered with boxes that James surmised was probably filled with junk.

"Great. Another fucking clutter room," he mumbled to himself. He searched the entire chamber but to no avail. He then searched through the other three rooms. The areas were all more or less gloomy, dusty and filled with useless junk that won't help him. James began to grow more and more desperate as his patience waned with each passing minute. "There has to be a damn flashlight somewhere around here in this fucking place!" he yelled in frustration, hurling books and papers onto the floor, making loud noises that caused the rats to scurry about in confusion and fear. James' remaining blood continued to boil over. "Just my fucking luck, there's no flashlight in this room, either." The fury caused him to forget his weakness, and he stormed down the hallway towards the first room he had passed up. It was the only one he had yet to check, and at that moment, ferocity caused him to forget the apprehension he had towards its' door.

James began to develop a nauseating feeling as he turned the knob to room 513. A warm gust of wind rushed past him as the entry opened. "What was that?" James asked himself as he entered the room. He felt like he was being watched by something the moment he stepped foot in there. "I... I'll make this fast," he whispered nervously. His voice sounded like the crackling high squeal of a scared twelve-year-old boy just hitting puberty

He began his search of the dimly lit chamber. James quickly darted towards the cabinet first and began to search it. He did not want to stay in this place for too long. James opened up all four cabinets back-to-back. He was disappointed to find that they all contained cobwebs, dead mice, and thick mats of dust. There was nothing of use contained inside them. He then began to search the aged desks' drawers.

All three of them were searched, and again, James came up short of a flashlight. All he found was more documents on the staff and patients who had worked and lived in this hospital. “Okay, one last place to check,” James said, but a glimmer of something shiny reflected in the dim light. James looked down at what looked to be an old, rotten tin box on the ground that was next to the front-most desk. He bent over and grabbed the tin container and placed it on the desk. It was a partially rusted-out lunch box. Like everything else in the building, it had clearly not been touched in a long time.

The side of the lunch box was dull, almost blood-color; James assumed that at one time, it was a brilliant red. The cartoon adorning the front was faded and nearly flaked off. He placed the lunch box on the desk and unclicked its’ two silver hinges. *Pop, pop!* The sound of the two locks rang loud throughout the room. James opened it hoping to find a flashlight or, at best, a box of matches but neither option was inside the box. Instead, the lunch box contained another cassette tape. There was not enough light to see what was actually written upon it. As James grabbed the tape, he heard an eerie shriek spring out from the hallway. The clamor sounded as if a piece of heavy furniture was being dragged across the floor. James mustered up the courage to walk towards the room’s entrance. As he made it to the open door, he peeked his head out into the hallway. James looked down both passages, but he saw nothing; the hallway proved to be empty. As he walked back towards the desk, he heard the loud shrieking sound again. This time it sounded closer. James turned around, slammed the door closed and locked it. He walked over to the desk furthest away from the door; the light of the hallway barely illuminated the room through the door’s window. After catching his breath, James pulled out the cassette player from his burlap sack. *Okay,* he thought to himself, trying to still his heavy breathing. *Let’s see what’s on this tape.* As he ejected the first cassette out of the player to insert the new one, his heart continued to race.

James sat back in the old chair and placed the cassette player on the desk. He stared at the device for a few seconds, hoping that this cassette would provide some clue as to how he could get out of this place. The room was quiet. James pressed the Play button with his thumb. The cassette player buzzed and hummed, the gears began to click and grind. James sat still, eagerly anticipating what he was about to hear on the tape. After about a minute or two, a familiar voice emerged from the little machine.

CHAPTER 18

"Hello. This is Dr. Philip Brookside. I am the head psychiatrist here at St. Mary's Hospital. Today's date is March 23rd, 1988. Today I will be recording another one-on-one session with patients 0388901 and 0284581.

I am going to start with a man named Harold Reeves, patient number: 0388901. Harold is a 28-year-old white male. He is a former manager at a grocery store chain. He resided with his wife, Mary, in a one-bedroom apartment on the corner of 8th Street and Dove Lane. Harold is six-foot-four and prefers to wear his long, blonde hair in a tight ponytail.

Harold suffers from multiple personality disorder, violent outbursts, and schizophrenia." James listens intently as the sound of a door swinging open can be heard on the tape. A man grunts as he walks into the room. *"Hello, Harold. Harold, please have a seat"*

"A'ight, Doc Man," a gruff voice said, followed by the sound of the couch squeaking, the man apparently making himself quite comfortable.

"So, Harold," Dr. Brookside asked. *"Do you know who I am?"*

"Yeah, you that doctor who talks to all the wackos 'round here."

"Well, technically speaking, I am a psychiatrist. Now, do you know why you are here, Harold?"

"I have no fuckin' clue, Doc." James could picture a smile emerging from the man's sun-tanned face.

"You are here because you killed your wife, Harold." There was a sound of scribbling into a notebook.

"Listen here, Doc, I di'nt kill my wife, okay?! So if that's all you need, then I'm leaving!" Harold replied, frustration taking hold in his voice. The pen sounded as if it were scratching across the notebook now; perhaps Dr. Brookside was unnerved at the man's presence.

This guy sounds like a mobster. Maybe he grew up or has family in New York? James thought to himself.
"Harold, you may go if you can answer me one question."

"A'ight, Doc. What'cha question?"

"Harold, what year is it?"

James heard the man on the couch let out a curt laugh. *"Come on, Doc. The year's 1923."* James could tell the man had a sort of cockiness about him.

"I'm sorry, Harold, but the year is actually 1988."

"You wrong, Doc! It's 1923 and I know it's 1923." The man was growing very angry, now.

"I'm sorry, Harold, but you're wrong. It is not 1923, it is 1988." More heavy note scribbling. *"Why do you think it's the year 1923, Harold?"*

"Simple, Doc. I just did a job for Al Capone last Tuesday. It was a hit on this two-bit loose lip fucker named Jack. Loose Lip Jack, they always call 'im. Capone was afraid the guy was gonna go blabbin' to the cops about something or other, so I got asked to whack 'im. So there, Doc, it's 19-fuckin'-23."

As James continued to listen to the conversation, he wondered to himself if Dr. Brookside's badge was one of the three that he might need to unlock the main door. *"If the Doctor's badge is one of the ones I do need, it has to be lying somewhere in this place, I'd think,"* he said quietly to himself. *"Unless, of course, he takes his badge home with him. If that's the case, I might be screwed."* James wondered where Dr. Brookside's office might be located.

The brass doorknob behind him because to rattle and slowly turn. James didn't seem to notice; he was still too deeply involved with the recording.

"I am sorry to tell you, Harold, but it's not 1923. You never worked for, nor knew, Al Capone," Dr. Brookside said. *"You are here because you suffer from multiple personality disorder. You have schizophrenia, you have violent outbursts, and now, I would safely say I could add to your case file that you suffer from delusions. Harold, you are locked up in this hospital because you killed your wife."*

"No, that's not true!" the man on the couch screamed. *"I would never hurt my Mary! I loved my wife!"* There was another squeak on the leather couch; Harold had evidently stood up. James could picture the man again, waving his arms about him as if pleading with the doctor. *"I loved my wife, Doc. You've got to believe me. I would never hurt Mary. Never."* Another sound; Harold sat back down, arching his back to sit upright. *"I love my wife, Doc. You have to believe me. I would never hurt my Mary."* The man began to quietly sob.

Dr. Brookside, still listening, scribbled some more into his notebook. Harold seemed to be transforming from his make-believe mobster persona into a scared young man who had no idea what was going on.

"Alright, Harold. Okay. I believe you. So, Harold, if you didn't kill your wife, do you know who did?"

"Yeah, I do. It was this guy, you see."

"A guy?" Dr. Brookside sounded curious. *"Well, do you know who this guy was? What did he look like?"*

"I can't say."

"You can't say, Harold, or you can't tell me?"

"Doc, I can't tell ya because if I do, he'd kill me."

"I had another patient, just a few months ago, that told me something similar. She told me that if she said his name, he would kill her."

James pictured the man's eyes growing wide. *"Yeah... yeah, that's right, Doc."* It sounded like Harold was wiping his hands on his pants, drying off the sweat.

"Can you describe to me what the man looked like?"

"Yeah, Doc... I... I think I can do that. He's... he's tall and he has these long, boney fingers. He has dark, hollow eyes like you were looking into an eternal void. Those eyes. Those eyes... they can show you your worst fears."

"So, have you ever looked directly into his eyes?"

"No, I haven't." James pictured Harold making the sign of the cross, grabbing his gold necklace and kissing it.

James didn't notice the medical gauze wrapped around his head slowly being removed. Whatever was taking the wrappings off, it was doing it so carefully so that James would not be disturbed. The tape recording came to an abrupt stop, clicking as it did. James popped open the door to the cassette player and flipped the tape over. Side B began just as Side A had. It was silent at first, but then, the conversation between Harold and Dr. Brookside continued. This time, however, it was difficult for James to make out what was being discussed; it was as if someone had attempted to muffle the words.

James was about to adjust the volume on the tape recorder when suddenly, something caught his attention. James raised his head as he thought he heard a whisper. "Amber? Amber, is that you?" he said.

"Don't be silly, James," he consoled himself. "It can't be her. She is at home with Liz. You're just hearing voices in your head. Your mind is playing tricks on you. Get yourself together."

Something grabbed the back of James' head and forcefully shoved his face into the wooden desk. The impact was so loud it had echoed throughout the building.

CHAPTER 19

"What the fuck was that?!" James screamed as he leaped out of the chair, holding the back of his head. He turned to look behind him. The hair on the back of his neck was standing on end. "Who! Who's there!" he growled, standing with fear in his eyes looking around the dark, empty room. The audiotape was still playing but James wasn't paying attention to what was said. The only noise James was hearing was his own heavy breathing. The dead silence made the room feel even more unnatural than it had already felt.

There was a loud screech coming from behind James. It sounded as if a sharp razor blade was grinding against a metal pipe. The sound was so loud and ear-splitting that James grabbed the tape recorder from the desk, along with his cane and burlap sack, and bolted out of the room.

James ran down the hallway as fast as he could with only one good leg, not looking back to see what, if anything, was behind him. He stopped just a few feet away from the stairs. "What the fuck just happened?" he asked himself while trying to catch his breath. James could feel his heart beating fast in his chest. He thought he could hear faint whispers surrounding him. "Who's there? Who?!" James demanded. He peered down and realized that he was still holding the tape player in his hand. He raised it up to his ears. A slight smile came across James' face as he let out a chuckle. "This damn thing was still playing the whole time," he said in amazement.

He turned the device off and put it back in the tan burlap bag, then draped the sack around his right shoulder. As James closed the bag he heard the heavy, thunderous footsteps.

The stomping was so heavy that small, white flakes of dust and asbestos were falling from the ceiling. The ground, ceiling, walls; everything shook violently as if the hospital were caught in the middle of an earthquake. James turned his head slightly to the left and gazed down the hallway. He attempted to see what was making the entire building shake. He couldn't see anything but a long, empty, terribly lit hallway. The hanging lights were swaying, now, in perfect sync with one another. They illuminated the grim walls with creeping shadows as they shook to and fro.

The noise of heavy footsteps was getting louder and louder as they ventured closer to James. He wanted to see if something was about to come out of one of the doors. He gazed around the dark passage but couldn't make out anything. The building shook even more; debris continued to cascade toward the ground. James thought that the racket was coming from the floor above him. The clamor hit the ground with such force that a glass window inside the nearest door shattered. Seemingly millions of tiny shards showered upon the nearby ground. James' face turned pale white in horror as footprints were emerging from the dust upon the tile floor. They were so deep and large that no human could have made it. The prints resembled those of horse's hooves.

"What the hell could be making these?" James asked himself as he began to experience double vision. He rubbed his eyes to regain his focus; more footprints were littering the ground by the second. Each step left the ground broken and cracked as the prints etched themselves into the tile floor. James then realized that the imprints stopped halfway down the hall. Two more hoof shapes appeared on the floor, James' eyes focused intently upon them.

He realized that whatever this thing was, it was facing him. It now seemed to be jogging towards James. He quickly opened the door and made with way towards the sixth floor, slamming it shut behind him as he reached his destination.

He could still hear the noise getting louder with each passing moment. Frightened that he would be caught and killed by the entity, James made his way into the first room he came across. He rushed inside, trying to escape from whatever was stalking after him. In his panic, James failed to notice that there was no number on the door. "Okay, okay, that was not real. It couldn't have been real. It's just my imagination getting the better of me," he sobbed out, trying to calm down. He was breathing heavily to the point of hyperventilation; the excitement started to make James feel weak and dizzy. "I've lost a lot of blood since I've been in this place. I don't know if I'll make it out of here to see Liz and Amber again." James' wounds had begun to clot over, but with the mass amount of blood lost it was a miracle he was able to breathe. "Also, I haven't eaten or slept in God knows how long. I think it's safe to say my brain is playing tricks on me. I'm seeing and hearing things. Shadows look like people. I'm hearing voices. Amber, Liz, I'm coming home. I promise. I'll find a way out of this place. Have a little bit of faith and give me the courage to get out of here." James was trying to convince himself that it was all in his head. "I need to find those badges and the torn pages fast. I need to leave this fucking place. What room am I in?" James looked around at his new surroundings. He had yet to explore this floor.

While searching the room, James ran into an open metal cabinet door, hitting his right shoulder. "Ah, fuck, that hurt," he cried out angrily as he grabbed his shoulder. "I can't see a fucking thing. Some God damn light would help." He slammed the cabinet door shut. Still searching around the room in the dark, James bumped into what he thought was another desk.

He stooped over to see if it had any loose drawers. As he was feeling around it, he realized that this was not a desk but a short cabinet. The felt at first as if it were made of wood but he couldn't immediately tell. James squatted down to open the cabinet doors. The rusted hinges squeaked as James swung them open.
A rat squeaked as it jumped out at James, causing him to fall back on his ass. James laughed for a moment then he started to rummage through the cabinet's insides.

As James searched the inside the cabinet, all he could feel was thick dust, cobwebs, and dead bugs. "This is disgusting," James said, still passing his hand throughout the dark cabinet. "Huh. What is this?" James asked himself. "It feels like a hidden compartment. Let's see if we have any luck here." *Wow, this is very tight. I can hardly fit my entire hand in this tiny opening.* James rummaged around the opening when he came across something rather familiar. "What is this?" he asked himself. "It feels like it might be metal or steel but I can't fully reach it yet." The unknown item was buried deep in a small compartment. James stretched out his fingers. "Just about got it!" he said as he rolled the metal object into his hand. "Yes! Yes! I finally found myself an old flashlight."

James felt around for a switch but could not find one. Inspecting the device further, he discovered that it had a wind-up crank attached to it. "Damn," he said, trying to move the handle. "This stupid thing is stuck..." he said. The crank finally gave way and began to move. "There. Shit yeah. I got it." The flashlight let out a howling noise and James twisted the handle, faster and faster. When it finally turned on, James remarked, "Shit, this is bright" He stood up, waving the lamp back and forth. It lit up the entire room with ease. James noticed an old painting hanging on the far wall. It looked to an old farmhouse on a hill, with a horse on the foreground, the night sky in the background.

A person was riding the horse, but James could not tell if it was a man or woman as the canvas was faded and cracked with time. The corner of the painting featured a slight rip upon its' surface. James looked around the room and found more paintings in the same condition. "I bet they looked nice back in the day," he told himself.

He came across a few old, tanned folders laying on top of a white, cluttered plastic table. "Nothing I can use here," he said to himself. "I need to go and look for those pages and badges." As he panned the flashlight towards the door, the beam of light caught the outer trim of what looked to be an old nurse's jacket. James walked towards the coat; he removed it from the hook on the rack it hung from. Pinned to the top right collar was a name badge.

"Samantha Longstreet," it read. "Huh. She was a Certified Nursing Assistant." James turned the badge over. Centered on the back of the badge a faded word written in permanent marker. Below the worn text was a magnetic strip. "Maybe this is one of the three badges I need to for that door. It looks pretty worn out. I hope it still works... Hell, I hope the door still works." James placed the nurse's badge inside his bag with its' other contents. He re-cranked the flashlight as it was beginning to dim. "I see the light only lasts a few minutes," he said as he took out the map to see where the next mark could be. "Okay, there is one close to me. It appears to be in room *613*.
The closest one to me now is down the hallway to the left according to this map." James was now starting to see multiple images on the map that blurred into one another as the double vision began to take hold once more. "I... I think I'll go check out the one on this floor," James said. He closed his eyes for a moment to let the effects of the vertigo pass. After a moment, the symptoms passed, and James left the room.

As he walked down the long corridor, James began to hear what sounded like terrifying screaming and crying echoing throughout the hallway. “It’s in my head, it’s all just in my damn head,” James kept on telling himself as he pressed on. The screams were getting louder. James turned around to see what was behind him. As he panned the flashlight from left to right, James saw nothing but empty halls.

“You see, James? There’s nothing back there. It’s just some old doors, a stained floor, some unwashed and broken windows. Sure, a few rats are running along the floorboard, but you’re all alone,” James told himself as he turned around. Eventually, he made his way down the hallway into the target room. He looked at each door he passed, reading the names on each one. James paused for a second. “Hello?” James shouted, his voice a little shaky. He could see standing at the far end of the corridor a female patient. She was dressed in a white, crumpled up, stained white gown facing the door on the left side of the hall. James began to walk towards the woman when two orderlies emerged from the door, grabbing the woman and dragging her back into the room. Both men were huge and wore dark blue, short-sleeved shirts with matching pants. One of the men had long, jet-black hair, pulled tightly into a ponytail. The other was bald and clean-shaven.

“I thought this place was empty,” James mumbled as he pulled out the map to double-check which room was circled. One of the men looked directly at James, then the three figures disappeared into the room without making a sound. “Okay,” James told himself, ignoring the scene before him, “it’s the fourth door to the left. Wait a second… that’s looks to be the same door that the woman and those two orderlies went into. Maybe they can help me get out of here.” James put away the map and headed for the door. As he passed the first door James’ stomach began to growl. “Fuck, I’m starving and sleepy.” He let out a huge yawn. “I need to find food and a place to rest.”

As he made his way past the second door James heard a familiar sound. The thundering footsteps echoed the hallways once again, followed by what sounded like a heavy metal object scraping on ceramic. James turned to look behind him and, to his horror, saw tiles being broken before his eyes. The floor was now being cut into by something huge that James could not see. He turned around and tried to run but, tried as he might, he could not escape whatever was trailing him. His mind raced with images of what could be after him. They ranged from a malevolent poltergeist, a grotesque giant, and even an unfathomable demon. The bottom tip of the cane skid upon the floor and caused James to fall hard. He grabbed the cane and quickly pulled himself back onto his feet. A burst of maniacal laughter engulfed the entire level of the building.

“What the fuck now!” James yelled as he continued to run towards an uncheck door.

“Run, run all that you want, little rabbit,” the apparition taunted. “There’s nowhere to hide, nowhere to escape. All you can do is run, run, run. I will have you soon, soon, soon and then the fun will begin, little rabbit. Run, little rabbit, run, because here I come.”

James was frozen for a moment in unadulterated fear, thinking about what – or who- was making its’ way towards him. Images of Liz and Amber flashed through his mind. James finally snapped out of his trance right as a huge iron, blood-soaked blade came barreling down the corridor towards him. His eyes grew wide with fright as he caught a glimpse of what was after him. James opened the door and ran into room *604* as the thing came charging forward. His heart was beating fast; his skin turned pale white. “What the fuck was that?” James asked himself, trying to steady his own breath. His shirt was soaked with sweat. James closed the door and locked it.

He then leaned his back against the wall and rested for a moment, trying to rationalize what had just happened. “Okay, okay. Calm down, James,” he asked of himself as he closed his eyes, trying to relax. James was still breathing heavily. “That was not real, that couldn’t have been real. I am just hallucinating. Yeah, that has to be what it was, a hallucination brought on by a multiple numbers of things,” he assured himself.

CHAPTER 20

James opened his eyes, shining his flashlight into the room. "Okay, I should be safe here for the time being. So, I guess I'll start looking for another torn page," James whispered to himself as he began to search the room. He searched the small cabinets on the left wall as well as the tall ones in the back of the room. There was nothing useful to be found here; more old files, more aged paperwork. He searched the desk in the front of the room hoping to find something. The room was silent except for the sound of James' heavy breathing. The room began to change shape as he walked further inside it. "What... what is going on?" he asked with fear trembling in his voice as he tried to pry the words out. The walls, floor, ceiling, chairs, desks; everything in the room suddenly burst into flames. As the chamber burned all James could do was watch. Everything erupted into an inferno and melted towards the floor into piles of ash. Just as quickly, the remains of the destroyed room transformed into an eerie, run-down, roach-infested hospital room with faded, stained porcelain tiles. The blotches on the walls formed a brown-red mixture. In the center was a hospital bed.

Small lights were shining down upon the hospital bed. They were dim and yellowed with time but were bright enough for James could see an older nurse sitting next to the bed. A woman in her mid-twenties laid on the mattress with her legs spread apart, naked from the waist downward, propped as if she were about to give birth. As James focused more on this woman, he could see that it was his wife, Liz. James rubbed his eyes in complete disbelief. He looked around the room and noticed there was a clock hanging on the back wall, several feet above the bed with its' faceplate shattered. It read 12:45 pm: the exact time of his daughter Amber's birth.

“What is going on here?” James asked himself. “It’s just like the day Amber was born. The clock in the delivery room was also broken on that day... but this was thirteen years ago.”

“I must have blacked out again. This time I must be a dream about my daughter’s birth,” he mumbled as a slight smile curved upon his lip. A nurse dressed in white scrubs and wearing a mask on her face suddenly walked up to James. “Hello, sir, I’m so sorry but you can’t be in here.”

“But I’m her husband, the father of the child she’s about to have,” James told the nurse.

“Oh, I’m so sorry, sir, my apologies. Please come with me to your wife’s bedside.” The nurse grabbed James’ right wrist and brought him to his wife’s bedside. Liz’s complexion was a dreadful mess. Her hair was matted, drenched in sweat. Her skin glowed a bright red as Liz was crying and screaming in pain.

“Liz, Liz, I’m here, Liz, I'm here,” James assured his wife, holding her hand.

“Oh God, James, it feels like I’m dying.” Tears rolled down Liz’s face.

“Its okay, hun, I promise. The pain will be over after you just give a few more good pushes.”

“I... I can’t!” Liz screamed as she felt her cervix stretch and rip the more she pushed. A loud, painful shrill echoed throughout the room.

“You’re doing great, Mrs. Callaway,” the nurse told her in a pleasant voice, examining Liz’s waist to judge her progress. “Great. Your cervix is at eight centimeters now.”

“So, is she ready to give birth?” James asked.

“Almost,” the nurse replied. “Her cervix has to be at least ten centimeters for the baby's head to safely pass through.” Liz screamed out in pain again as she felt her body ripping apart.

“You’re doing great, just keep pushing,” the nurse assured Liz.

“You heard the nurse, Liz, you’re doing fine. Just keep it up.” James said. Liz yelled again as she put forth a great effort. Her face was now a bright red and her breathing was getting heavier with each passing minute. A pool of blood along with small splats of fecal matter gushed out onto the lining of the bed. “AHHHHH! Fuck this shit, get it out of me, fuck, it hurts so bad!” Liz screamed. James grabbed his wife's hand tighter, trying to comfort her. “You’re almost done, hun,” he said, but his words fell on deaf ears. Liz looked at James in a way that sent fear racing to his core. Her eyes glared with pure hatred.

“Don’t you ever touch me again!” Liz barked at James.

“I can see the head coming, miss,” The nurse said with cheer in her voice.
“You hear that, Liz?” James said happily. “She can see the head. Just a few more good pushes and our little girl will be born. Come on, love, just a few more.”

The baby’s head was now beginning to emerge. The slimy, bloody mucus membrane covering it popped and began to ooze from Liz's inner thigh down onto the bed. “Okay, Liz. One more good push, okay? Now, push hard!” James implored his wife, close to shouting. Liz took a deep breath and pushed as hard as she could. Her eyes squinted tight as she gripped the bed, screaming at the top of her lungs.

“Good job, ma’am, I have the baby’s shoulders,” the nurse told them as she started pulling the baby out. James kissed his wife on her forehead. “I am going to go watch our daughter being born. I want to be the first person she sees as she comes into the world.” James peered towards the bottom of the bed. The smile that once graced his face soon turned downward as he saw the baby.

“What the fuck is that?” yelled James in horror. The nurse forcefully ripped the newborn out of Liz’s body, causing her to pass out from the pain. James could see the torn umbilical cord dangling from his wife as blood and fluids began to pour all over the bed. The smell of rotten birth discharge filled the room. James' eyes began to water as a rusted iron taste began to coat his mouth.

“Would you like to see your daughter now, sir?” The nurse asked James as she presented the newborn to him in a clean rag. Loud crying rang forth from the newborn.

“No… that… that thing is not my daughter,” James stated with fear in his voice.

“Oh, but it is, sir,” the nurse told him, a sickly smile gracing her eyes and face.

“No, that horror is not my daughter. That is not Amber!” James yelled as he took the crying newborn and threw it against the wall. The rags fell away from the baby. James stared at the grayish, withered, decayed, and deformed corpse still fresh and pulsating. Its’ eyes were fused shut. Black bile began to spew forth from its’ mouth.

“This is not real, this is not real, I’m in a nightmare,” James said, quaking back and forth, eyes wide. He ran over to his wife’s bedside.

"Liz, Liz, wake up... something terrible happened to our daughter!" James said to her. His eyes were fixed on the abomination that laid upon the ground just a few feet from him. James shook his wife once more, screaming in her ear. "Liz, Liz, wake up, Liz."

James looked down at his wife a second time. The body lying in the bed was not of his wife but was that of a rotten corpse. The dried, decaying skin was melting off of her face like hot sticky caramel. Coagulated blood oozed from her hollowed-out eyes. The body was so thin and gray her bones were protruding through whatever skin she had left.

James took a few steps back in horror, cupping his hands upon his mouth as he tried to make sense of what was going on. "This can't be real; this is not real. No, none of this is real," he kept repeating like a madman.

"Come, my dear. Take a look at the fruit of our love." The corpse of his wife turned its' head to look at him. Vomit spewed out from her mouth as it talked. "Yes, James... take look at your daughter," the nurse said. Turning to look at the nurse, James saw that her lower jaw was missing. Fresh blood was flowing from her missing appendage. "What the hell?" James implored, frightened, jumping backward. The nurse hissed; blood sprayed from her mouth everywhere. Her tongue flapped around unnaturally as she spoke.

In the shock of what was going on, James keeps on repeating to himself, "No. This is not real." He backed himself against the door. The decaying baby picked itself up onto its' feet and began walking towards James. The light in the room flickered on and off as it swayed its' fragile body back and forth. The creature did not stop crying as it extended its' arms out; small hands were opening and closing as if it were trying to grab the air.

Black goo oozed from every orifice of its' body. As it waddled towards James it began to piss blood onto the floor. He quickly grabbed the doorknob as he watched the thing continue to walk towards him, crying incessantly. James couldn't help noticing that the rest of the ripped umbilical cord was still attached to it, dangling onto the floor. The shriveled umbilical cord was blackish-gray and possessed hints of dried blood.

The baby was just a few feet from James now. He quickly tried to open the door, only to fumble with the doorknob in his panic. "Stay the fuck away from me!" James yelled as the door opened, causing him to crash hard onto the hallway floor. James continued to inch backward until he hit the opposite wall. Now, facing the door he just emerged from, James broke down, sobbing uncontrollably. "It wasn't real, it wasn't real," James kept repeating to himself, his voice utterly broken.

CHAPTER 21

James pulled his legs tightly into his chest, wrapped his arms around them, and buried his face into his knees. He was still thoroughly traumatized by what he had just witnessed. Hands shaking uncontrollably, he mumbled to himself, "G-get ahold of yo-your, yourself, J-James. That was not... not real. That wasn't your wife. That... that THING... it wasn't your baby. This place is messing with your head." Tears ran down his face, soaking his beard. "I have to... to find the other torn pages. After I collect all the pages and ID tags I can finally get out of this place. I can finally see Liz and Amber again... forget all about this place." He took several moments to collect himself. Once he was sufficiently calmed down, he pulled himself back up to his feet with the help of his cane and the wall. James then wiped his eyes with the inner part of his shirt's collar. Clearing away the tears, he then took another deep breath and reached into his bag.

James took out the map and looked to make sure that there was a marked room on this floor. The old, hand-drawn map showed a room circled in red being on the sixth floor. James looked at the map and, using his index finger, he traced a path starting from the stairway through the hall, past the wall with a crack in it. It came to a stop upon the room circled in red. "So, if I followed the map right, then the room is..." James whispered to himself. He peered around. There was a room directly across where he just came from.

"Shit," he said, his voice sounding monotone, dead. This was where he needed to be. His heart was once again racing with fear as he approached this new entryway.

After giving himself a little talk of encouragement, James opened the white, dust-caked door and shined his flashlight into the room before him. To James' relief, this room looked nothing like the hellscape he just escaped from.

It was not a disgusting hospital room with corpses inside; No, this room was a regular physician's office. James panned the flashlight slowly, sweeping the beam from right to left. He spotted a table laying against the right-hand wall. This table was once used by doctors to prop their patients up for a routine checkup, James surmised. He then looked over all the walls. There were several medical diagram pictures. Glancing his flashlight upon the room's door, he noted a tattered patient pain chart gracing its' facade. Only one of the diagrams in the room was still intact; the others looked to be covered with mildew and falling apart. As James searched the chamber, he came across a short desk in the corner opposite the patient stand.
Scanning the desk with his light he could see a few empty medical beakers, all featuring pictured taped upon them. There was also a full box of latex gloves. This desk only had one drawer at the bottom. James opened it and looked inside. There were a few ink pens, some tape, and a balled-up piece of paper. James grabbed paper an un-crumbled it.

The paper had the number written on it: *65*. "Yes!" James shouted in triumph as the paper had the second set of numbers he needed for the building's front door. "Okay then, just a few more items to get then I am out of nightmarish place." A slight smile began to emerge upon his face.

James exited the room and began to make his is way towards the stairwell door opposite of the one he used to reach this level. As James walked down the corridor, he couldn't help but notice that there was still no sign of daylight.

"Okay, I know most of the top floors are deeply covered with overgrown vines, but even then, I should be able to see some small amount of sunlight trying to get through," he wondered to himself as he walked past a brown-stained window. After James passed the window a bloody handprint appeared on the lower part of the glass; judging by the size, he figured it probably belonged to a child. It disappeared just as quickly as it had manifested. Walking down this corridor, James remembered that he was close to Dr. Coffin's office. He decided he would go looking for that Doctor's ID badge.

After several minutes, James finally comes across room *615. I guess now is the best time to look for that badge,* James thought to himself, his inner voice sounding to himself as a childish whisper. A cold shiver ran down his back. "I'll just go in, grab the badge and leave. Simple enough, right?" he told himself, trying to find the motivation to grab the door handle. When he placed his hand upon it, he noted it was covered in a brownish-red, sticky substance. "What the fuck is this?" he asked himself as he wiped the mysterious substance onto his right pants leg. James tried to turn the handle but it seemed that the door wouldn't budge. "Great," said James, sighing. "Just fucking great. This damn door is stuck. I'll have to find something to pry the door open." Upset but undaunted, he quickly turned around and proceeded from the direction he had originally come. As he came to the corner of the hall, his stomach began to ache and growl with hunger pains. The hurt was becoming unbearable; he needed to find something to eat. "I don't think I'll last much longer... I need to find something, anything." James fell to one knee. Another surge of pain shot through his stomach. Just as he was about to stand back up, a rat scurried by. It had red-tinted eyes and matted brown fur.

The hunger was so overwhelming that James had momentarily forgotten about his damaged leg. He dove onto the floor to catch the rat, nabbing it on his first swing.

The rodent was biting and scratching at him trying to break free as it frantically squirmed and squealed. James immediately applied pressure onto the rat's neck and rib cage, squeezing it to death as it bit his long teeth into James' hands in vain. It thrashed and squealed wildly but soon the life had completely drained from its' body. "There!" James said moments later as he felt the rat's neck snap in half.

James inspected the dead rat closer; he didn't seem to mind the blood running down his hand from where the rodent had bitten him. He began to think about just how he could cut the rodent open to dig the meat out. "Well, since I don't have anything sharp on me, or in my bag, I guess I'll just have to rip him open with my teeth," James mused. He held the rat up to his mouth with both hands and placed its' back into his mouth. James could feel the matted fur of the rat tickling his tongue. With his eyes closed, James bit down as hard as he could. Fur and skin became lodged between James' teeth as he pulled, hard as he could, ripping large amounts of fur and skin from the creature's lifeless body. Warm blood and scraggly fur began to fill his mouth. James spit the fur, skin, and blood on the ground next to him. He repeated this a few times until the rat was now a pink, skinless, bloodless corpse. His hands were now stained in a dark crimson glow as it dripped the rat's fluids onto the floor.

James bit down hard on the raw, pink, bloody flesh. He ripped chunk after chunk with his teeth and chewed the tough meat. The warm blood of the rat mixed with James' saliva in his mouth almost reminded him how he used to order his steaks: medium-rare topped with A-1 steak sauce. He continued to pull at the carcass with his teeth, ripping gory chunks off the rat's bones. He let the blood race down his beard as he continued to eat away at the rat. After several minutes there was nothing left but a pile of torn fur, ripped skin, and red fluid stains adorning the ground.

James wiped his mouth on the sleeve of his left hand. "That was awful… but it should sustain me for the time being." As James got back to his feet the speaker system once again kicked to life. "Tsk, tsk… Eating rats now? My, oh, my, how the so-called righteous have fallen. What would your little Amber think of her Daddy devouring diseased, worm-infested rodents?" The man's voice was obscured by a wave of static buzzing.

"You leave my family the fuck alone, bastard" James yelled in anger. "What the fuck do you want from me?"

There was a silence in the hallway that seemed to last forever, but after a few moments, the voice reappeared. "We want you to suffer for what you've done to us."

"We?" James yelled, confused. So, there are multiple people behind this? "I didn't do anything to you or your friends," yelled James. He waited for a response back but heard nothing. He continued to walk down the hallway towards the stairwell with a puzzled look on his face, trying to figure out what the guy was talking about. He found his way to the stairwell door. He was about to open it but stopped. James thought that there might still be something on this floor he can use to help him get Dr. Coffin's door unstuck. "Maybe there's some kind of metal object lying around one of the other rooms," he thought as he moved away from the door. He began to trace his steps, turning down the corridor he had passed a few minutes ago. As James was passing one particular room he suddenly stopped in his tracks. There, lying in front of the door, was a massive pile of debris. What… What's going on? That wasn't there moments ago, James thought. What happened? Why is this pile of debris laying here, and who placed it there? There was no wind; the air condition hadn't been turned on since he arrived at this place. So, how did it get there, then? It could have been one of the others, trying to fuck with me further.

James figured that he was the only one on this level of the building. If there was someone, he would have seen them by now. He shrugged it off, finally figuring the pile had been there the entire time but that he must've overlooked it. He shined the flashlight over the pile one last time and pressed on.

After a minute, he came upon a door on the right-hand side. "I haven't checked this room yet," he said as he entered the room. James searched for something, anything, he could use to pry Dr. Coffin's door open, but he came up with nothing useful. James walked out of the room.

James was now weary as the hallway was now in total darkness. The lights hanging from the ceiling were not just turned off; James shined the flashlight down the dark hallway and noticed shimmering reflections of broken glass on the floor. The walls now had a darker, yellow-colored tint on them with a black liquid-like substance pouring forth from random orifices. "Wh-what the fuck happened here?" James gasped. The black goo looked as if it were pulsating, almost like a heart beating. James couldn't help but stare at the nefarious slime as he walked down the corridor. He went back to room 615. "Dr. Coffin's office," James said in a low voice. An eerie chill ran up his back as he felt something- or someone- standing behind him. He grabbed the doorknob again and was relieved to find that it was no longer stuck. James looked behind him to see if anything was there.

"There's nothing there, man. Come on, get a grip, you're losing your mind in this place," he told himself, feeling his heart beating as if it were about to explode from his chest. He slowly opened the door. "Last time I tried to open this... it was solidly stuck in the frame. Who unjammed it?" James wondered.

CHAPTER 22

James turned on the flashlight as he entered Dr. Coffin's office. "I can finally see a little bit better now thanks to the flashlight," he told himself as he began to search the room. "Wow. I never realized just how messy this Dr. Coffin was until now." James noticed the doctor's coat hanging up on a metal coat rack on the right side of the door. He walked up to it and had some trouble trying to take it off of its' hook. After a few tugs, the coat finally managed to come free. It was old and dusty, caked in various stains with several moth holes lining its' sleeves and back. The dried red stains on the faded white coat made James think that the doctor may have been a surgeon.

He started to search the coat pockets for Doctor Coffin's ID badge but had no luck finding it. "This sucks; no ID badge," James murmured as he tossed the coat on the floor. He rechecked the two file cabinets. While looking through the same files from before, James came across something rather interesting. "Huh, what's this?" he said as he pulled a newspaper article hidden under one of the folders. James unfolded the crumpled yellow sheet then placed it upon the desk to straighten it. Sitting down with the flashlight shining on the snippet, James began to read.

The New Jefferson Gazette

Monday, October 22, 2007

KILLER FINALLY CAUGHT
by Crystal Davenport

After several long months of investigation, countless leads, and an extensive manhunt, the New Jefferson County Sheriff's Office arrested a man in connection to last January's gruesome murders at The Grand Harbor Hotel. The suspect, Dr. Jason Coffin, has been charged by the State with two counts of first-degree murder and is currently being held in the county jail without bond. Both counts carry the possibility of the death penalty.

On Friday, April 13, 2007, New Jefferson deputies responded to a call regarding the bodies of two female victims, later identified through DNA evidence as Dr. Coffin's wife, Lauren Coffin, and their daughter, Amanda Coffin, in the basement of the hotel. Police were able to dispatch an arrest warrant once county forensics determined that fluid found in the women's vaginal canals belonged to Dr. Jason Coffin.

Detective Mark Smith determined that both women were raped and then killed. "We found significant lacerations on the inners thighs of both his wife and daughter, as well as skin cells underneath their fingernails, clearly indicating an intense struggle against their assailant."

New Jefferson deputies raided Dr. Coffin's office at St. Mary's Hospital on April 28. Their investigation turned up extensive documentation detailing a series of horrific attacks multiple patients suffered over the years at St. Mary's.

The hospital has undergone multiple lawsuits concerning patient abuse by families since Dr. Coffin took over the day-to-day operations of the facility in 1972.

After initially cooperating with detectives, Dr. Jason Coffin went on the run on the morning of April 16. He was apprehended by Canadian officials while attempting to cross the U.S.-Canada border via Detroit's Ambassador Bridge around 4 pm on October 17. An attentive CBSA officer discovered that Jason Coffin was in possession of stolen Canadian and Indonesian passports. U.S. Department of State officials filed extradition paperwork soon afterward, and Dr. Coffin was returned to New Jefferson County several days later. The case has been referred to the jurisdiction of Justice Raven O'Connor. The date of the trial has yet to be determined.

As James finished reading the article, he couldn't help but to feel a pit in his stomach. "I knew he was probably a sick fucker, but wow," James remarked, placing the page face down upon the desk. He then peered into the middle drawer. There was a keyring with only one key on it. *I wonder where this key fits,* he wondered as he placed it on the desk.

Inspecting the bottom drawer produced a small, cardboard container, wrapped in brown paper. James removed the covering and opened the box. Dr. Coffin's ID badge soon emerged from it. "Yes, I found it!" James shouted happily as he examined the newfound article. It looked the same as the one he already possessed, save for having a different name plastered on its' face. James placed the badge in his burlap sack. It was then he noticed something hand-written on the back of the newspaper clipping.

The main electronic metal door in the front is on a different electrical breaker. The breaker is found in the basement. The key to the breaker is located on this desk. If anything goes wrong, use the key to turn the power to the door back on. The note was, curiously, signed Dr. Coffin.

"Ah, so that's what the key is for," James told himself, grabbing the key. Placing the key into his bag, he pulled out the map and looked at it once more. He realized as he studied the drawing that someone had sketched an image of the basement level. "Why would someone make a map of just the basement?" he wondered.

The door burst open. A tall, rather chubby, middle-aged man with short blonde hair wearing a faded coat identical to the one hanging in the room yelled, "I told you I would find you. You have escaped my experiments one too many times, now. You will pay!" James quickly sprung to his feet. The mysterious figure rushed towards him.

"Hey, look, I have no idea what the hell you're talking about. I woke up in this place. I am trying to get out so I can be reunited with my family." James slowly starts moving around the desk, inching his way towards the door. The crazed, wide-eyed look on the strange man was fixed on James. "Who... who are you?" James asked, slinking towards the door. The desk was the only thing keeping the two men separated.

"I will be drag you to the basement where you will be dealt with," The man shouted at the top of his lungs.

James quickly glanced at the name on the badge the man had clipped to his coat. *Dr. Jason Coffin.* "What? You're Doctor Coffin?" James blurted, stunned. "But how? I have his name badge in my bag. You are in prison, or maybe you're dead. How?" He quickly decided he was dreaming or hallucinating. Or, perhaps, this was a prank sprung by the people who locked him inside this place.

James tried to reason with the so-called doctor. He didn't notice that the room was starting to change. The office began to morph, walls bursting into flames. The air was covered in ash, glowing in a fierce yellow-red. The walls became dark, gray stone in parts, as other sections morphed into a chain-link fence topped with barbed wire. Loud screams of torture pierced through the surrounding darkness. James' eyes finally adjusted to the scene before him.

All the furniture in the office was disintegrating. James could see several pairs of hands reaching through the fencing as they cried out for help. Their fingers were covered in dried blood and their skin was shredded. Their digits lacked the presence of fingernails.

Horrified, James made his way closer to where the door had been. He could see other patients' limbs shackled in thick, heavy iron restraints and chains. Their naked bodies were covered in four-inch deep lacerations. Their screams of pain were so unbearable to James that he had to cover his ears.
James noticed a tall, beastly creature with a whip in its' hand appear. The creature had to be at least fourteen feet tall and weigh over five tons in solid muscle. His body was covered in a mixture of long and short brown hairs. The smell of wet animal fur filled the entire room. Four perfectly shaped ram horns protruded out of its' head. Each time it lashed its' whip, serval of the people chained to the wall gained new cuts across their bodies. The hilt of the whip was a thick black leather with eight thin wires flaring outward. Each little wire themselves possessed four-inch-thick razor blades approximately two to three inches apart from one another. As James looked the weapon over, each blade had appeared longer and sharper than the last.

The so-called Doctor began convulsing uncontrollably, his clothes melting into his skin. His entire body turned to grotesque gelatin. His eyes, nose, and mouth had been replaced by a distorted pink dripping glob.

The man stopped shaking and turned to James, deliberately walking toward him. James now realized that this thing was not human and that it was still changing. He could see that this Doctor-creature now possessed neither a face nor arms. James finally grabbed for the door with his back while the humanoid abomination rushed him. Turning, James opened the door and fell face-first into the hallway floor. The thing fell upon the floor, puss-filled boils spilling their contents everywhere. James' eyes began to hurt in a migraine-like pain. The door slammed itself with a heavy clank.

CHAPTER 23

James' heart racing uncontrolled. He couldn't believe what he was witnessing. He knew now without a doubt that something evil was lurking in the old, abandoned hospital with him. More than ever he needed to get out of this place. The abominable glob creature had vanished. Not waiting for it to return or for the door to reopen itself, James made a hasty retreat. As he made his way towards the stairwell, he reflected upon everything that had happened in the hospital. "Am I hallucinating due to the amount of blood I have been losing, or is the hospital actually haunted?" he asked. A small smile quickly draped over his face but was wiped away as he heard a door squeak open behind him. James was still a bit shaken up about what had just happened. His eyes grew wide with fear as he realized that the door that just opened was for the room he just escaped from. Dr. Coffin's office was now stood wide open, emitting a foul smell from within its' bowels. It reminded James of baked human flesh. James' eyes began to water as he heard what sounded like children laughing in glee.

James was now frozen with fear and dared not even make a move. He went completely numb to the situation surrounding him. Thoughts of Liz and Amber raced to the forefront of his mind; images of his honeymoon night, of Amber learning how to ride a bike, his first day working for the lawn firm. Tears slowly fell down his cheek as he watched, one by one, the other doors slowly start to open.

James pointed the flashlight down the poorly lit hallway. He could see the tiny charcoal-blackened hands of children reaching forth from the walls. Their dried skin was flaky, sulking off the skin with ease; these were severe burn victims. The more James gaped, the more he could see the bright orange lines veins running along their wrists.

James quickly realized that their bodies also began to emerge in a similar disposition.

“My God,” James said, horrified, staring at their charred faces. All of the burnt childrens’ eyes had a frightful yellowish glow emitting from them. Some of them sported terrifying smiles that appeared to be carved on with a surgical instrument. One by one they began to leave their enclosures and stalk along the corridor’s floor. Each entity twisted and convulsed with every step. “My God! Is this hell?” James whispered to himself. He turned off the flashlight hoping the figures would disappear; instead, the hallway only filled with glowingly terrible eyes.

James grabbed the stairway handle. Without taking his gaze from these horrid apparitions, James slid into the opening. The pitter-patter sounds of their feet slapped the tile floor as the figures picked up speed, spiriting towards James. He slammed the door shut and, ignoring his leg pain, leaped quickly down the steps.

James passed the next level down, pausing briefly to consider the door. “I think I'll go down to the fourth floor, but I’ll open this up a bit to make it look like I went here. Hopefully, this throws whatever’s following me off my trail.” The door on the platform above creaked open. James did not want to wait around and see what his pursuers would do or even if they had already spotted him. He opened the fifth-floor door, flew down the staircase, and entered the fourth level.

“Okay, I think I’m safe now… maybe,” James said as he shined his flashlight down the corridor. “Hey, I remember this floor.” He tried to put recent events out of his mind and focused on the task at hand. “This is the floor that has the room with those empty bathtubs. I think I’ll go recheck that area. I might be able to find something in that room now that I have a flashlight.”

He made his way back to room *413*. The horrifying thoughts of getting caught by the children seemed distant in his mind. James' mission now was to escape this place. As he re-entered the room he began to look around. This time, he had held a better visual of the room with the help of the flashlight. "This is really a bathroom. It's well outdated and run down," James told himself. The flashlight's glow reflected off of the white porcelain tiles in the room, brightening the chamber up even more. He could now see that several titles were missing from the walls, cracked and chipped. James passed the light over the room to get a better look at the bathtubs. They were all stained with time but none appeared to be particularly damaged. James passed his gaze back towards the walls. "I wonder if the tiles are just broken with age or if they were deliberately taken off," James said to himself as he stared at the pockmarks. "There has to be something useful here. I hope."

As he continued the search, his flashlight caught sight of something underneath a bathtub towards the back of the room. "What is that?" James asked himself as he made his way toward the tub, shining his flashlight. "Still empty. That's good," he sighed, allowing a faint smirk. "With everything that's going on I was almost expecting something to jump out at me. This place probably isn't haunted. I'm just losing my mind, that's all." The smile turned into a hearty chuckle.

James located some debris behind the bathtub. "Yes!" James shouted excitedly as he found the third torn page. He quickly reached in his bag and pulled out the other pages. "Now all I need is that last page and the last badge, then I can get the hell out of this damned place."

While putting the Pages back into the burlap sack, something on the wall began to appear in his line of sight. "Oh, what in God's name is this?" James said, shining his flashlight upon the wall.

Letters were suddenly materializing before him, styled as if they were written in blood. “What the hell is going on?” Beads of sweat started to gather on James’ brow as he started to read the words. The words all appeared backward.

DEXIF ERA UOY NEHW EVAEL LL‘UOY. DEXIF ERA UOY NEHW EVAEL LL‘UOY. DEXIF ERA UOY NEHW EVAEL LL‘UOY

“This makes no sense,” he said out loud when he realized what the message was. “You’ll leave when you are fixed? What does that even mean?”

James bumped into one of the bathtubs as he made his way back to the hall. “Damn it, that fucking hurt!” he cried, holding his left thigh. As he rubbed the side of his pants he realized that his pants were now soaking wet. “Huh?” he asked himself, confused. “There’s no water in these bathtubs.” He shined the flashlight on the nearest tub only to discover that it was now full of dark brown liquid. James blinked, still confused. *Who filled this bathtub up with dirty water? Could it have been one of the men who put me in here?* he contemplated. James, with the assistance of his cane, knelt downward. He dipped two fingers into the dark liquid. “I know this thickness. This isn’t water!” he shouted in horror as he immediately pulled his fingers out of the tub. “I… I know what this is… but I can’t believe it.” He shined the flashlight onto his index finger. “Its BLOOD!” James jumped back onto his feet.

He frantically began pointing his lantern onto all the tubs in the room. “They’re all… they’re all… BLOOD! Gallons and gallons of blood!” James started to panic. The bathtubs began to violently rock back and forth, sending a large amount of blood spilling on the floor and coating every surface in the room. James tried to head towards the door but the slipperiness of the ground and the vibration of the tubs rocking back and forth had caused him to fall.

He dropped the flashlight and, fumbling for it, grabbed the lamp and shined it at the door. “There’s a straight path towards the hallway,” he muttered to himself. The bathtubs continued to shake as if the room were rocking from an earthquake.

They developed cracks, covering James with their gory contents. James quickly made it back to his feet and bolted for the door, cane in hand. He did not dare to stop and look back behind him. He had not cared about the sounds of the bathtubs moving. His focus was solely on the door and of exiting the room. He reached the opening and dashed through it. The cane was caught upon a crack on the hallway’s surface, causing James to fall once again.

CHAPTER 24

James was freaking out about the vast amount of blood covering him. As he looked down toward his soaked clothes, he is surprised to find his clothes not only dry but clean. “What? Where is the blood? There was blood on me!” he shouted, confused, eyes wide with shock. He checked his shirt, pants, and the rest of his body again for any signs of blood. “How?” he asked in disbelief. “I watched the blood pour on me. I felt the sticky warmth of it hit my skin and my clothes. I know for a fact that I was drenched in blood. But then how...?” While to make some logical sense of what had just transpired, James soon remembered that he had found the third torn page. James quickly opened the burlap bag and pulled it out into the light. “Okay, let’s see what number is on this one,” he said with a smile, momentarily forgetting the latest episode of horror. There it was, in bold, black ink: the number *37*. “Okay, then, just one more page to go,” he remarked as he placed the page back in the bag and pulled out the map.

Reading the map now James noticed that there was a second circle marked on the floor he was on. “It looks like the other marker is not too far from where I'm currently at. All I have to do is go down the hallway, turn right at the corner and walk until I reach the last door to the left. He tucked the page back in his bag and began walking down the dark hallway, flashlight in hand. It flickered with each step James took, fading from bright to dim and bright again. As he turned the corner, James began to feel week. His sight was becoming blurry again, his balance was shaky, his head felt as if a thick fog were descending upon it. James took another step forward and collapsed onto the cold, hard, filth-strewn ground. The flashlight hit the floor with a loud thud and rolled several feet away from James.

He attempted to prop himself back on his feet, but he was too dazed to make a successful attempt. The lack of nutrition had finally caught up to him, and the medicine injected hours earlier had fully worn off. James felt as if he were about to pass out for good. A few tears traced his cheeks. “Liz, Amber, I am so, so sorry.” He closed his eyes and began to drift away. The sound of heavy footsteps interrupted his reverie. “Huh? Who is that?” he said, his voice filled with a rasp. With all his might, he opened his eyes to look at who was approaching him.

“Mr. Callaway, what on earth are you doing on the floor, sir?” The mysterious voice asked him.

“Huh? Who are you?” James replied.

“I am the night janitor, sir. You know me, I’m Mr. Nodum. Please, though, call me Xolyus. You should be up in your room, Mr. Callaway.” James looked up to see concern painted brightly on the black man’s face.

“Room? No, no, I have to get out of this place. I have to go home and see my family again. I… I collapsed out of weakness. Lack of food,” James told Xolyus. The janitor proceeded to help James back onto his feet. His vision was still a bit blurry; he struggled to take in the entirety of his surroundings. “Come on, Mr. Callaway, I’ll bring you back to your room.” The janitor's voice sounded calm and smooth.

“No, I have to get out of here. I must get out of here; my wife and daughter are waiting for me.”

Xolyus Nodum looked at James with a frown. “You will leave when you’re fixed, Mr. Callaway.”

“What did you just say?” James replied, his eyes wide with horror.

“You were in a very nasty wreck. Your car was totaled. Your right leg was crushed, you sustained a nasty head injury as well. That is why you’re here, so the doctors can fix you, Mr. Callaway. So, let’s get you back to your nice, quiet, cozy room.”

Xolyus’ face was graced with a bright, friendly smile now. James collapsed on himself once again. “Like I said, you need to be fixed,” the night janitor said as he helped James to his feet. “Are you feeling alright?”

“No, I feel like I haven’t eaten for days. That’s why I’m feeling so weak. I need food.” James quietly sobbed.

“Well, before I bring you back to your bed, let’s get you something to eat. How does that sound?” asked the janitor, a beaming smile plastered on his face.

A smile finally crossed James’ face. “That sounds great,” he said. The two men made their way down the hall. James tucked his cane under his right armpit as his left arm draped around the janitor’s shoulder. As they walked down the hallway, James’ sight became clearer. He looked Xolyus over. “Huh. You don’t look like a janitor...” James said to him, trying to pry his mind from the thought of food.

“Well, I am. It’s the best way for a man like me to earn a hurt back, y’know.” The man’s English, while slightly accented, was nevertheless perfect. James continued to talk with the man. Xolyus Nodum stood six feet eight and inches tall with short, gray hair and stubble indicating he was trying to grow a beard. The man was outfitted with a dark green jumpsuit. Based on his accent, James suspected he may have been born in Africa.

“I thought I was the only one here,” James told the janitor.

“No, sir, you are not. This hospital’s filled with people, man. That nasty head wound you have must have caused you to have amnesia. Your new medication is probably causing you to hallucinate. Those quacks upstairs need to adjust your dose.”

“New medication?” James asked, silently confused about how a janitor could know so much about his condition.

They stopped in front of two dark green doors. “Where does this lead to?” James asked Mr. Nodum.

“This is the cafeteria, of course,” the man replied.

“But I thought the cafeteria was on the first floor.”

“We're on the first floor,” Xolyus said with a grin. “Don’t you pay attention to the signs?”

“But I thought I was on the fourth floor?”

“They just gave you the medication a few hours ago, Mr. Callaway. You probably forgot where you are. You think you’re in one place when, truthfully, you are somewhere else. Now, let’s go to the cafeteria and I’ll see if they have anything left over from today’s dinner, okay?”

“Okay,” James said. “Thank you.”

They entered the cafeteria. Xolyus helped James to the middle of the nearest circular table. James sat down and laid his cane next to him. "Wait, I dropped my flashlight in the hallway!" James utter as he shifted himself in the chair.

"Sir, your flashlight is in your bag. You got to chill, now. Please sit down and relax. I'll go see what kind of food is still left in the kitchen, okay?"

Xolyus disappeared into the kitchen. James opened the bag that was slung onto his shoulder. "My flashlight!" James said, surprise "Here it is."

"I have good news, Mr. Callaway!" It was the janitor. He held a full plate of food as he walked towards James. "They had spaghetti with grilled chicken breast today, and there was still some in the refrigerator. I went and warmed it up for you, sir."

Xolyus placed the plate of food in front of James. The spaghetti looked and smelled amazing as steam poured from the top. It was a large mountain of hot pasta smothered in a rich, thick, creamy red sauce and two well-sized, big, juicy chicken breasts. "Oh, man, this looks almost too good to be true. Thank you so much, Xolyus," James said as his voice perked up.

"No problem, sir. I knew you would approve. It's truly a plate to die for. Now, you just relax and enjoy it. There is plenty more in the back if your still hungry," Xolyus Nodum stated, his pronounced smile ever-present.

James picked up the fork and knife that was right next to him. He began to cut the long pasta into smaller pieces and twirl it around his fork.

He made sure to scoop up some of the thick, delicious red sauce with it before putting it in his mouth. The hot food burnt his tongue slightly as he placed it in his mouth, but James didn't care. The taste of the dish brought tears to his eyes. The pasta melted in his mouth as the rich and vibrant flavors kissed his taste buds. "Wow, this is amazing!" James said out loud as his mouth was full of spaghetti. He could taste a bouquet of wonderful flavors as they danced on his tongue. The meal contained hints of garlic, rosemary, sage, onions, red peppers, and parsley as well as the sugar, salt, and pepper. James cut into one of the chicken breasts with his knife; it was lovingly smothered with parmesan cheese. Hot steam escaped from meat with every slice James made. The hot, flavorful juices ran out of the chicken and onto the plate.

The tender white meat of the chicken breast looked and smelled very inviting. James couldn't wait to place a cut piece of chicken in his mouth. Just like the pasta, the tender meat melted in his mouth. The perfectly seasoned chicken was so intoxicating to James' taste buds that he slowly savored every bite. It contained hints of salt and pepper, the sweet but mildly hot heat of paprika, the strong but subtle hint of garlic powder. James could make out the taste of olive oil. Even the parmesan cheese tasted incredibly delightful.

"Are you enjoying the food, sir?" Mr. Nodum asked.

"This is so incredibly delicious," James replied as he kept stuffing his face. He paused only to drink a few gulps of water. *I must appear as if I'm eating like a man possessed,* James thought to himself, *but hell, I don't care.* "This is so, so very good."

James smiled as he placed his fork and knife on the empty plate, visibly satisfied. The janitor walked up to James. "Looks like you enjoyed the food, I take it?" he asked James.

"Oh, it was so good. It reminded me of the dish my wife and daughter would make at home. Right down to the olive oil," James mused with a smile.

"Think you have any room for more?"

Wiping his mouth with a napkin, James replied, "Yes."

"Okay, Mr. Callaway, I'll be right back with another plate."

After a few minutes, the janitor came back out with another plate of spaghetti. "Here you go, Mr. Callaway," he said as he placed the second plate on the table for James. "Eat up. There's plenty to be had."

Just as he had done with the first plate, James tore through the contents with immense haste, devouring every last bit. "When I get home, I must have Liz make spaghetti-like this," he told himself, finishing up his second helping.

"Excuse me, Xolyus," James said as he called to the janitor.

"Yes, sir, what can I help you with?"

"Could I have just one more plate, please?"

"Yes, sir, of course. You must be hungry, just inhaling all that food like you are. Just let me get this empty plate out of your way and I'll bring you another right away."

"Thank you so much," James told him as the man picked up the plate. James watched as the janitor walked into the kitchen with an empty plate, returning soon with more.

“Huh, he must have already had it ready for me,” James whispered to himself. Xolyus placed the food in front of James and he began digging in for more.

Just like before, James destroyed the plate of food. The janitor walked up as James polished off the remnants.

“Freshening up your glass of water for you, sir.” James nodded his head.

“Why are you waiting on me hand and foot like you’re my butler?” James asked while still eating.

The old black man smiled. “Because you remind me of myself when I was your age,” he told James as he titled the pitcher of water and began to pour into James’ glass. “When I get a taste of something good, I always tear it up.”

“This plate of spaghetti is so good. I have to know what you use in your recipe so I can tell my wife. There’s something else in here that just takes it above and beyond what my family makes,” James said as he took a sip of water.

“Yes, of course, Mr. Callaway,” the janitor replied as his lip curled up. “Whatever you want, you got it.”

CHAPTER 25

The thin white wall that divided the cafeteria and kitchen started to crumble away as the janitor clapped his hands several times. James watched as yellow and white lights started to illuminate the back of the kitchen. It was a horrid mess. There were large, rusted, unclean pots and pans on the stove boiling over with a thick brown liquid. The walls were caked with dried, stale food. On one of the back tables were sliced old moldy bread. Flies were swarming around rotten slabs of meat; large maggots covered and writhed over the surface. James even spotted several roaches crawling on the counter and floor. He could not believe the state of the kitchen. “That is where my... my food was cooked?” He leaned over the side of the table to upchuck vomit.

“Would you like to see how your delicious spaghetti and baked parmesan chicken breast were prepared for you, Mr. Callaway?” Xolyus asked as his smile turned sinister, curling up his face and nearly reaching his eyes

“No!” James said as he stopped himself from putting another twirled fork of pasta on his mouth. A large spotlight clicked on and shined on a large white sheet hanging in the back of the kitchen. The sheet fell to the ground, revealing James’ wife Liz strapped to a large pasta grinder. Every time the handle turned, Liz screamed in horrifying agony as her lower half was stretched and shredded into long thin pasta ribbons. The rusted metal blades of the grinder cut deep into her, ripping and tearing the flesh from her body like a paper shredder.

Coming out on the other end of the pasta grinder was a nightmarish mixture of bloody skin, organs, tissue, and bone resembling the vague form of pasta noodles. His wife's cries were only muffled by the loud buzzing and grinding sound of the blades, humming as they turned.

James' eyes widened in horror as he watched Liz's body ripping apart. "Liz, no! Oh, God, stop this now!" James cried with fear and anger as he locked eyes with his wife. He could see the pain in her eyes. "Why... why is she here?" James asked the janitor as he stumbled over his words.

"It's simple, Mr. Callaway. You wanted to see how we made that delicious, mouth-watering meal you have been so happily stuffing your gullet with. So here it is, Mr. Callaway."

Xolyus laughed hysterically. James looked down at his plate. The pasta was transformed into a grotesque, blood-curdling mess made of his wife's flesh. The thick, rich sauce was now a pool of dark, coagulated blood that covered the skin noodles. "What the fuck!" James yelled between bouts of vomit. He looked at the baked chicken breast.

"Is this even chicken?" he asked himself, unsure as he poked it with the fork.

"Yes, and no," the janitor replied. "You could say, anyway, that it is one hundred percent breast."

"Br... breast?!" James asked in fear.

The janitor pointed to another white sheet lit by a spotlight. Just as he was pointing, this garment also fell to the ground, revealing James' daughter, Amber. She was suspended mid-air at a forty-five-degree angle.

Her arms and legs were spread out; her wrists and ankles were chained. Her young upper body was exposed, breasts hanging down. “Amber!” James yelled at his daughter as tears ran down his face. He couldn’t do anything but watch as his daughter was lowered onto a meat slicer. The high pitch back-and-forth grinding sound of the blades twisting on was almost enough to muffle the painful screaming of his daughter, her breasts filleted with each swing.

The razors tore through Ambers’ soft flesh like butter. After every cut she was hoisted back up a few feet above the machine, her torso covered in blood. She had only two large circular wounds where her breasts used to be located. Shredded skin and tissue barely hung from her like, resembling ripped sheets of notebook paper. Her breasts regenerated after every round of slicing. James watched in immense in horror as both his wife and daughter were being cut into ribbons.

“Yes, every time you wanted more of the so-called chicken breast, apparently succulent pasta, this is what you were getting... well, we had to source it from somewhere, didn’t we? What better place to get a home-cooked meal than from the members of your own household? Surely you agree with me, sir.” Xolyus’ voice was at an eerie calm.

James looked down at the half-eaten chicken breast. Right before his eyes, the juicy, tender white meat morphed into a shriveled, bloody slice of human flesh. The once baked parmesan now took on the appearance of think, dry, rubbery skin. Smatterings of blood oozed out of the cut-up meat.

“I’m... I' m sorry. I’m so sorry. Please forgive me,” James whispered to his wife and daughter as he then begged the janitor for them to be free. Xolyus just smiled at James as he pressed a button on the wall next to him. “What's that, you want another plate, Mr. Callaway? Oh, of course, sir, coming right up.” His voice was audibly frenzied.

The two machines started up again. Loud buzzing and grinding sounds filled the kitchen. James couldn't move to help his wife and daughter, try as he might. He was helpless; all he could do was watch his wife and daughter being cut up like pigs in a slaughterhouse. Liz looked down at her husband with tears in her fearful eyes. "James, help me, James, please" she cried as the grinder once again started up. James cried out his wife's name as he shut his eyes tight.

"Ohh... no, no, no, Mr. Callaway. You WILL watch this!" It felt as if something were prying James' eyes open, yet the entity doing so remained unseen. He was being forced to watch his wife's body being lowered into the machine once again. Her blood-curdling agony cried throughout James' head.

"Daddy, Daddy, please help me!"

"Amber!" James yelled as he turned his head, tears flowing from his eyes as he did so. His daughter locked her eyes with his as she, too, was lowered into the machine. "Daddy, I don't want to do this. It hurts. I just want to go home, Daddy. Please, Daddy, I just want to go home." Tears flooded the side of her face.

The sound of the cutters spinning filled the kitchen once more. Ambers' eyes grew wide with fear. "Daddy, I'm so sorry, I'll be good, Daddy, please, I will be."

"I know you will be, love. Don't worry, we will go home little one. You, mommy, and I will go home together. Daddy will rescue you and Mommy and we will all go home." The blades sank once more into Amber's flesh.

Hair raising screams filled the room. “You fucking bastard, let them go! I demand you to let them go!” James was growing angry as the tears waterfalled down his cheeks.

“Now, now, little rabbit, we’re just getting started.” The janitor replied. Only now, he wasn’t quite the janitor anymore. The man's body started to convulse and transform, becoming taller and more deformed. His fingers grew into long, bony claws. Legs began to pop and break as they grew, and then, multiplied. His knees broke inward, facing backward along with his feet. The dark green jumpsuit he was wearing melted into his black-skinned shell. Xolyus, or whatever the hell he was, then started to rip large, bloody chunks of skin and hair from his head, revealing a gray, mossy mane of hair that now hung slightly over the porcelain mask covering his face. His eyes were hollow and dark, with reddish-black smoke emitting from the corners. The demonic creature was now just a few feet from James, staring him down.

“What... in all of Hell... what ARE you?” James asked it nervously.

The thing spoke not in words, but in a burst of loud, hyena-like laughter as it pounced towards James. He quickly raised his hands to defend himself from the creature as a white flash overcame the entire room.

CHAPTER 26

"James? James?" a mysterious female voice echoed. A quick flash of lightning illuminated the single bedroom apartment. The sound of a car alarm filled the midnight air.

"James, James, hey James."

"Yes, hun? ...What time is it?"

"It's eleven o'clock at night. Are you okay?"

"Yeah, I'm fine," James replied, rubbing his eyes, half-cocking a smile. "Yeah, it's just my mind wandering." His forehead was covered in perspiration. He took the bottom of his nightshirt and wiped his entire face dry. James was sitting in a small chair, his laptop placed on a foldout table. The remains of a microwave spaghetti dinner sat pressed against the wall.

"Take a break and come to bed," Liz said. "You've been on your laptop for nearly seven hours now and, besides, your daughter is kicking. Come and feel." Liz was flipping through channels on the TV to see what was on.

"I can't right now," James said, flipping through some paperwork. "I have to win the case. I have already lost four big cases since I joined the firm. Bryan Lunsford, Kristal Rheim, Zell Harlan. And of course..." he continued, yawning, "the Rooney case. I was their attorney. I let them all down. All the evidence said that they were..."

"Guilty," Liz interrupted. "You forget, love, I work for the same firm as you. That's how we met in the first place."

"All I asked you to do was come over to my place so we can go over the Lunsford case."

"Yeah, and came I did," Liz told him, quietly giggling. "I haven't left your place since."

James turned off his laptop and crawled into bed with his wife. He rested his head on the right side of Liz's well-developed stomach. "I can feel our daughter moving," James told her as a smile came across his face.

"So, what are we going to name our little girl?' Liz asked.

James thought for a moment then sat up. "How about Winter?"

"Winter? No, I hate that name." Liz exclaimed.

"Okay, okay, what about Sam?" Liz stared at James when he suggested it.

"How about Martha?" she said, smiling.

"Martha, like from the Batman vs Superman movie?" James said. "No, I'm not naming my daughter after a comic book character that dies." James and Liz tossed names back and forth; some of them were just for laughs.

"How about Bobby Jo?" Liz suggested, giggling.

“Oh, yeah, and everyone will call her B.J,” James said. He moved to the edge of the bed.

“I really need to win this case, you know,” he said, abruptly changing the mood from playful and cheery to stressed and under pressure. Liz placed her hands on her husband’s shoulders and started to rub them. “You are the smartest defense attorney I know. So what if you lost a few cases? That will happen from time to time.”

“But I-”

“No buts,” said Liz, turning her head towards James so that their eyes met. “You will win this case, I know it,” she told him, embracing him in a hug. James grabbed his wife.

“I need to provide for you and our daughter. I don’t want her growing up in a rundown place like this.”

“She won’t,” Liz said, sternly but with a sincere smile on her face. “Besides, I can tell that your daughter is a little fireball just like her dad.”

“Thanks, hun,” James said as a smile came across his face.

James turned his head to the television. It was turned on but the sound was low, almost muted. He grabbed the remote and raised the volume.

“Breaking news: a fire broke out in the Warehouse District causing a candy store on the corner of 9th and Walter Street erupted in flames. We go there live to John Guillerman with the latest. John?”

"Thank you, Sarah. As you can see behind me, Mary & Bill's Candy Shoppe caught on fire just over an hour ago. Firefighters were quick to arrive on the scene and are still fighting the blaze. A few of the neighbors are out here, now, and they've all told me that this old fashioned candy store is held dear in the hearts of this neighborhood. Chief Cortez of the Fire Department stated that the blaze started in the kitchen, stating that a shop employee told the Chief he accidentally dropped ambers from his lit cigarette onto some nearby baking grease. Four people were in the building at the time, including two people living in the apartment upstairs. I'm told that everyone got out safely and no one was hurt. Police and Fire officials will be performing a thorough investigation in the coming days. Back to you, Sarah."

"Thank you, John. We will bring you an update to this story on our regular newscast at 7 am. Good night."

The originally scheduled program came back on the screen. James mumbled to himself for a few minutes; his expression was the one he always held when he was in deep thought. After a few minutes, he turned to look at Liz. "Hey, how about the name Amber?"

Liz paused for a moment. "Amber," she mumbled to herself while rubbing her stomach. "I like the name and I think she likes it, too," she replied, smiling as her left hand jumped due to Amber's kicking. James got up off the bed.

"Where are you going?" Liz asked him.

"I have to win this case. I am going to go back and sit in the chair. I think I have a few more hours left in me."

Suddenly, the power went out. "Oh, well, that's just fucking great. My show was about to come on, too." Exclaim Liz, half-jokingly.

"Looks like I'm gonna have to go reset the damn fuse."

"Well, be careful, James, and... hurry back, okay? I'm kind of feeling in the mood," she said with a smile.

"I will," replied James, a sly grin creeping on his face.

On his way out the door, James grabbed a small flashlight. With the light on he made his way towards the breaker box. Less than two minutes went by until James reached the box outside in the backyard. As he opened the metal panel, fighting against the rain, James began to think about how life would be for him and his growing family once they were living in their own house.

"Okay, let's see, which fuse blew again?" James said, shining the light into the box. "Ah. I see it. It's this one." He grabbed onto the switch and flipped it. A huge electrical arc flashed, and white light engulfed the small backyard. The force of the blast threw James to the ground.

CHAPTER 27

James woke up back in the hospital hallway he had originally collapsed on. His vision was blurry as he tried to focus on the dim ceiling lights hanging above him. "What happened? Was... was any of that even real?" James asked himself as he sat up. His head was spinning; an intense pounding invaded the back of his eyes. James wiped a finger along the bridge of his nose. He still wondered if what took place really did happen or not. As his vision came back into focus, he noticed that the light shining on the ground was from his flashlight.

"I remember walking towards a door marked on the map," he told himself, "but I tripped and fell hard. My flashlight bounced out my hand as it hit the ground. But I also remember a janitor by the name of Xolyus walking towards me and helping me up. He brought me to the cafeteria where I ate several plates of spaghetti and baked chicken breast, but it was... it was... oh, God!" James' hands started to shake and tremble as memories of what just transpired began to flood his mind. "It couldn't have been real. It's too... But I... I still can taste the flesh and blood in my mouth. The flesh and blood of my wife and child. I was eating them." James began to sob, devastated at the memory. He sat on his knees, his head looking down at his palms. His hands were shaking uncontrollably. "I can still hear their cries and screams as they were being mutilated. My daughter begged me to save her and... I couldn't... even move. But, before that, I fell down right here." James took a deep breath and collected himself. "No! That wasn't real, my wife and daughter are safe at home, they are waiting for me."

James pulled out the map from the burlap sack and check the mark on it more time. He was still a bit shaken at what he remembered. James grabbed his cane from the ground, which was laying just a few inches from him, and got back to his feet. He walked over to the flashlight on the ground. James bent down and grabbed it. Just as he stood back up, the PA system crackled back to life. "Are we having fun yet, James?" the voice asked, monotone, dead-like.

"You will pay for what you did to me. Who are you?!" James yelled.

"You will know soon enough, James," the male voice said before the speaker once again fell silent.

James proceeded down the hall. As he turned the corner, he thought he had seen a shadowy silhouette of a man caught in his flashlight. James rubbed his eyes with his right hand, trying to focus on what the beam had caught. There was nothing there. No dark, shadowy spot. Just an old dirty wall. James was growing tired of looking at the same grungy, slimy, dust-encrusted walls.

"My vision must still be a bit blurry," he said as he walked up to the door marked on the map. It had already been slightly propped open. James read the name etched into the stained glass window of the door. *Doctor P. Brookside.* James gripped the handle, opened the door, and walked entered the chamber. The beam of the flashlight lit the office with just enough light for James to see. The room, although in desperate need of cleaning, was exactly how James had pictured it from listening to the tapes.

A large and faded black leather couch pushed against the back wall, next to a tall bookshelf in the room. In the right upper corner of the room was a small cherry-wood desk that was cluttered with books and paperwork.

Silverfish retreated, scattering when James shone his flashlight on the tomes. James noticed another bookshelf with just as many books on it on the left wall. He walked over towards that bookshelf to examine it. "If I were one of the people entrusted with a key badge in my office, I would hide that badge inside one of my many books," James said to himself as he began rummaging through the shelf. He peered through book after book, flipping through pages, looking for a sign of anything secreted away. All the while he couldn't shake the image of the janitor out his head. "I wonder who that guy was or if he even really existed," he said.

James came across an old, thin notebook. It was markedly different from the rest of the books on these shelves. It was brown and leather-bound with a thin, red lace wrapped around its' cover. There was also a yellow piece of yawn stitching crisscrossing the binding. James flipped through its' contents; the first couple of pages were left blank. As he made his way towards the middle pages, he came across a weird style of writing. "What the hell is this?" James whispered to himself, wondering just what the strange writing could mean. It looked almost as if it were formed from the symbols of an ancient religion. There were only five pages filled with the strange runes.

All the pages afterward were blank just like the first few pages. James put the book back on the shelf, brushing off the strange writing as nothing important.

He took a step back to reexamine the shelf. As he looked at each row of books that were placed upon it, James soon realized that each row of books on the shelf featured the same colored covers. Every row except for one: the bottom shelf. The row of books on the at the bottom featured dark green covers, except for one book in the middle. It was reddish-brown. James grabbed the book and started to look through it.

As he flipped the pages, a small folded letter fell out along with the last badge. James looked down at the letter. He closed the book and placed it flat down on the edge of the shelf, its' binder hanging off towards the floor. Stooping over and picking up the folded letter, wondering why someone would go through the trouble to hide it, James opened it and began to read, leaning his back against the bookshelf as he did.

I fear that my time working at this hospital is running out. I no longer feel the warm feeling for this place I once had when I first started working here. Throughout the years, the happy, friendly atmosphere had slowly changed into that of a frightening, hateful tomb. This place now feels eviler and eviler with each passing day. The once warm and friendly staff that work here have changed, and not for the better, mind you. Their demeanor, I fear, is no longer their own.

Dr. Coffin has recently installed a new type of electronic door in the main lobby, as well as a new surveillance camera system throughout the hospital. The only way to get into this new door to work is by inputting an eight-digit numerical code on the digital pad and scanning all three authorized badges. He said he has this door installed so that the patients could not escape. It would have been okay, but, he also had all but one of the exits to the hospital bricked up. An exit which only he knows the location of.

The only way in and out is now through the new main door. I hear strange chanting coming from down in the basement at night sometimes while I wait to be let out. I stumbled upon a book with strange writing while I was investigating the basement one night. A few of my patients have recounted to me very disturbing things; terrifying events have been taking place in the basement at night. These are frightening things that I have been strictly forbidden from discussing.

I have recorded a few of these sessions on multiple tapes and hid them throughout the hospital. I am afraid this will be my last day here. I don't believe I will be leaving this place alive after tonight. If you find this note and read it then you must get out. Don't get trapped in here like the rest of us.

Sincerely,

Doctor P. Brookside.

Taken back a bit by what he had just read, James decided to check the rest of the room for any more information on the hospital and Dr. Brookside. He checked the doctor's desk. Looking through the scattered mess of papers on the desk, James didn't manage to find anything useful. "What? That's odd," he commented when inspecting the drawers. "There is only one real drawer here; the other two are just for show," he said to himself as he tried to open them.

He opened the only drawer that wasn't false; it was the small one on the top right. It made a squeaking sound along its' track as James tugged at it. The well-worn plastic wheels were grinding on the rusted metal tracks. "Wow, this drawer needs lubrication, big time," James said. Inside it was shoved more papers and notebooks. He started to quickly look through each of the items he found. As James read through notebooks, he skipped pages and skimmed paragraphs. "All of these books concern the patients he treated. The loose papers scattered in the drawer are about the changes in the staff." James dug around more in the drawer. He came across another audiotape hidden in the back. "Huh. I wonder what is on this one?" James asked himself as he put the tape on top of the desk.

He rummaged throughout his bag to get the cassette player out. He placed the device down on the desk next to the tape. Opening the player door, he pulled out the cassette that he'd already listened to. He remembered well the name of that patient: Harold Reeves. Placing the new tape in the machine, he pressed the large Play button and waited.

CHAPTER 28

James sat down in the faded brown chair next to the desk as he waited for the audio. The tape started out as the previous two tapes had. There was a loud grinding sound of the gears humming as it ran, followed by a somewhat long, drawn-out silence. A familiar voice began to talk.

"Hello, my name is Dr. Philip Brookside. I am currently still the head psychiatrist here at St. Mary's Hospital. Today's date is August 11th, 1988. Today will be my last session with patient 0388901, Kelly Mailhos."

"Good afternoon, Kelly. How have you been?"

"Afternoon, Doctah B. A girl at lunch a few days ago, she tol' me her dad got sent to the kill table in person. She said he was on trial cuz of what he done, an' he kept givin' the officers different names."

"Sounds interesting." The noise of scribbling.

"So, Kelly, this will be our last session, Okay?"

"Okay," she replied, sadness evident in her voice. *"Why this be the last time, Doctah B? Did I do something wrong?"*

"No, not at all, Kelly. It is a personal matter that I'd rather not discuss, that's all. Let's instead continue where we left off from our last session, okay? Just lay back on the couch like last time."

Dr. Brookside goes through the typical motions of a hypnosis session. He assures Kelly that his voice is calm and smooth, all the while flipping through a notebook.

"Okay, Kelly, are we ready to begin?"

Kelly's voice was incredibly relaxed. *"Yes."*

"Kelly, do you remember what we talked about in our last session?" Dr. Brookside asked.

"Yes, I do."

"You wanted to tell me about the shadowy figure, and his name, correct?"

"Tha's right."

Dr. Brookside adjusted himself in his wooden chair for a moment. *"So, Kelly, can you tell me what his name is?"*

There was a long pause. Kelly was audibly breathing heavily. James could picture in his mind her eyes darting upward at the ceiling, then across to the open closet at the small wooden shelf, which was barely visible. She fixated on the darkness inside the closet.

Finally, she said, *"I don' think he'd like that, Doctah B."*

"Why can't you tell me, Kelly? You're safe in here."

"You know why," she said in a slightly deeper tone, nervous, her southern drawl melting away.

"You can't tell me because he would kill you if I did. Correct?"

"That's right, Doc. If I tell anyone his name, he will kill me." Though James could not see the patient, he knew without a doubt that Kelly's eyes did not move away from the closet.

"Kelly... Kelly?"

There was the sound of Kelly shifting on the couch, squeaking the leather as she did so. Dr. Brookside also shifted in his chair, grunting. James could tell something was going on in the office, but what, he did not know.

"Kelly..." Dr. Brookside implored once more.

Suddenly, she shouted, *"Stop it! That's not very nice!"*

James could hear Dr. Brookside scribbling so madly that he may as well have been ripping the pages with his pen.

"Kelly," he spoke, calmly. *"If you can't tell me his name, can you at least describe to me what he looks like?"*

"Yes... I can describe him to you, but I thought I already told you what he looks like?" she replied, confused.

"I might have forgotten that you told me. So, it's really just a refresh for my memory."

"Okay, umm... well, he's very tall, very tall and thin. His fingers are long and... thin like bone. He has long gray hair and it, like, looks like dried moss and his skin is dark gray, too. Usually. He can change."

"Change?" the doctor asked, hints of doubt in his voice. *"How would you say he can change?"*

"Well," Kelly said before drawing a sigh. *"You know like how a caterpillar can transform into a butterfly? Well... it's like that, but he does it quickly."*

All the while, Dr. Brookside's pen was scratching the paper, never pausing. James could only picture how mangled the notebook must look by that point. *"Kelly.. you do realize that this person you speak of, he's not real."*

"No!" she shouted. *"He is real and he killed my family. He killed my family. Not me. He killed them."*

"Is this man she's describing... is he the same thing I've been seeing around the hospital?" James whispered to himself. After Kelly mentioned his transformation ability, he wondered if the thing pursuing him was the same entity this girl claimed to have dealt with. A moth flickered past James' flashlight. "Huh... I haven't seen a moth in this place yet," he mused.

"Okay, Kelly, calm down and take a deep breath. Why do you think that people don't believe you?"

"Well," she said as she shifted on the couch again, *"Because that what he does. He makes you see stuff that ain't there. He even tricks you into hearing things too. After a while, you just question if everything's real."* She sounded afraid. James pictured the unseen girl pilling her legs into her chest, hugging her knees. The doctor's pen never stopped tearing at the pages; each stroke echoed loudly through the tape. James could only imagine how erratic the notes must have looked.

There was a momentary pause at the noise; Dr. Brookside must have put the notebook down. *"I think we should take a little break for now. What do you think, Kelly"*

"Oh... I think that sounds nice," she replied in a whisper.

The recording started to skip as it came to an end. James pressed the eject button when the cassette player clicked off. He looked around the room, checking if anything were present with him. "Good, I'm still by myself," he whispered to himself. James turned the tape over and pressed play, and after a few seconds, the conversation continued.

James continued to listen to the conversation, which picked up after the pair recording it had apparently finished their break. Dr. Brookside didn't ask any more questions about the entity haunting Kelly; the conversation turned toward lighter themes, about school, her favorite animals, foods that she liked. About five minutes in an eerie buzzing noise came through the speaker. "What the hell was that?" James said as the sound's high pitch rang through his ears.

CHAPTER 29

A stranger's voice came on the tape after a brief pause. It was different; a heavy rasp clouded every syllable uttered. The voice did not belong to Dr. Brookside or Kelly. It sounded as if it were a male, but James couldn't be sure. He wondered who this person was and where he had come from. James could also hear a very faint noise in the background. "What is that?" he asked himself, turning the volume up to its' maximum.

It sounded as if the noise were an old record player jamming away; the music of a full orchestra wafted through the air. "It... it sounds like... like elevator music!" James told himself, surprised as he turned the volume back down. Before he finished lowering the sound, the raspy voice said something that sent chills down James' spine.

"I will see you very soon, James!" the gruff stranger said to him in a crisp, clear tone. James' eyes grew wide, goosebumps covering every surface of his exposed skin. He was trying to think of who could have possibly been in the same room as Dr. Brookside and his patient. "I thought these sessions were just one on one?" he asked himself. James completely lost track of what the pair had been discussing.

He rewound the cassette tape to try and see if he could hear the message again. He could not find a hint of the rasped man's voice. When he pressed play, the tape started with Dr. Brookside and Kelly continuing the conversation they were having on 'A' side.

"What? Where is the voice that I heard a few minutes ago?" James said nervously. He checked the extent of the cassette several times for evidence of the man talking but to no avail.

He even flipped the cassette over a few times, thinking that it may somehow trigger the voice to appear as if it were part of a secret code. No luck. It was as if the mystery man was never on the tape. He continued to listen to the therapy session taken place. Eight minutes in, James abruptly stopped the tape at a part where Kelly told Dr. Brookside something that made James jump.

"Wait, Kelly. So, you are telling me that you see things on the TV that others could not see?"

"Yes, Doc. I'd be watching the TV with my family. We'd be looking at COPS or maybe The Simpsons. All of a sudden, he would be looking right at me in the background, waving at me. Everyone else in the room wouldn't be able to see him at all. The episodes just played like they were normal."

"Interesting," the doctor replied. *"So, when you say you would see him in the TV, do you mean like a reflection, or...?"*

"No, Doc!" Kelly's voice grew louder, panicked. James could hear her hands digging into the couch's leather. *"My family and I would be watching a show and... he would be IN the show. If it were a live show, he'd be there. If it were a cartoon, he'd be animated with the other characters. He'd be in the show for only a few minutes but I am certain it was him."* Her voice audibly trembled as she continued to speak.

"Kelly... do you think that maybe this guy you've claimed to see and interact with was just in your head? That he was a manifestation of guilt, perhaps." Dr. Brookside had stopped scribbling; it sounded as if he might have been chewing on his pen's cap.

"No! I didn't make him up. He's just as real as you or me!" Kelly began to cry. A loud knock echoed through the tape, and James inwardly pictured the pair looking directly at the closet.

"What the hell was that?" the doctor said. *"I thought I had left the closet door open?"*

"It was." Kelly's voice sounded frightful yet calm all at once as if she were resigned to a yet-determined fate. *"He closed it."*

"Who is he?!" the doctor demanded. *"Kelly, tell me his name."*

There more knocks rang forth, slowly and deliberately. It sounded as if whoever was knocking wanted to toy with the pair. *"Kelly, tell me his name,"* the doctor once again implored, his voice calm yet raised.

"I can't, Doc. I just can't. I didn't kill my family. He did it. I can't tell you his name." She was weeping incredibly now, her nose sounding as if it were ejecting molten snot. The closet door began shaking violently.

Dr. Brookside once again tried reasoning with the girl. *"Kelly, I cannot help you overcome this tragic part of your life and help you move on if you don't tell me his name."*

"Okay..." she said, composing herself. *"I... I will tell you his name."* The knocking turned into a beating, thundering increasingly with each stroke of force. James turned toward the closet door now, inspecting it, wondering how it was still intact after being so incredibly slammed. Just as suddenly as it had begun, the knocking ceased.

Kelly whispered a name under her breath. It was too low for the doctor and James to hear. *"I'm sorry, Kelly,"* Philip Brookside said, *"I couldn't make out what you said."*

"His name..." she hesitated. *"His name is..."*

"Yes?"

"Xol'hasan." Her voice was deep, as if it emitted from a void, as she perfectly pronounced the foreign syllables. *"Xol'hasan. Xol'hasan. His name is Xol'hasan."*

"So, that's his name... I see." The doctor once again proceeded to jot down words into his notebook, this time at a more leisurely pace.

"Yes. That's what he told me to call him," Kelly said, sheer terror drowning her voice.

"I see," the doctor replied. James silently lipped the name of her tormentor. *"Kelly. You do realize... this... 'Hasan' does not exist. He only existed in your head."*

"NO! He's as real as you an' me. Did you just forget what happened a few minutes ago? Did you not think that was real?"

Dr. Brookside placed his notebook on the desk. *"Kelly... and hear me out for a minute... but Kelly, I believe you actually have the ability of telekinesis. It would explain why strange things happen around you and why objects move on their own sometimes when you're nearby. You just don't realize that you're doing it."*

"No, Doc, I'm not doing this. I'm not doing nothin'. It's all Xol'hasan. He's doing this, not me!"

"It's certainly a rare ability, a lot of researchers don't even believe it's real, but I think..." Dr. Brookside's tone suddenly changed, sharpened with fear. *"WHAT?! Kelly... she's... she's... GONE?!"*

James heard the doctor jump his feet, stomping all about the office. *"Kelly... Kelly? Where are you? Where did you go?!"* Moments of heavy breathing, the sound of the closet door opening and slamming shut, rang through the cassette player's speaker. There was a loud, audible crack as if someone were flicking light switch repeatedly, followed by an intense scream. "What the fuck just happened?" James said, trying to contemplate the events transpiring through time.

There was the sound of a chair being violently shuffled. A moment passed, and Dr. Brookside's excited voice said, *"Where... where did she go?!"* James turned his head, seeing something out the corner of his eye. He could make out the faint outline of a shadow, shaped like a man, searching through the office. James rubbed his eyes; was this truly happening before him? The figure's eyes grew wide with shock, looking at the empty couch in the room. It appeared to speak, but the sound James heard came only from the tape recorder. *"Where DID she go?!"* Dr. Brookside's voice asked. *"She couldn't have left the room...the door, I locked it,"* the doctor's voice said as James watched the mystery figure walk towards the office door. *"I locked it,"* Dr. Brookside said again. *"Where could she be?"*

The shadowy figure, who James now assumed was Dr. Brookside himself, searched the entire room. Whatever it was looking for was no longer in the office. The figure was about to leave the room, presumably to inform the staff of what had happened, when it spotted something laying on the couch. James also turned to match its' gaze. A small, folded piece of paper had appeared in the middle of the leather couch. Both the figure and James walked towards it. The shadowed man picked the paper up, unfolded it, and began reading. Dr. Brookside's voice read the note out loud for the tape recorder.

"Kelly is mine now. You are next, doctor.

Sincerely,

Xol'hasan."

The shadow man stared at the letter for several, trying to figure out what to make of the note and the sudden disappearance of his patient. Just a few inches away from the note laid a girl's ponytail. *"That is Kelly's favorite ponytail,"* Dr. Brookside said, picking up the purple object, trying to wrap his head around what was happening. *"I-I still don't understand what happened here. Did she do this for more attention, is this one of her many multiple personalities manifesting?"*

James sat in the chair, listening to the tape and observing the shadowy figure, trying to also figure out exactly what had happened to Kelly. He contemplated who exactly this Xol'hasan entity possibly was. The tape clicked a few times and then abruptly ended. The shadowed man disappeared. Nothing but silence permeated the office now. James couldn't help thinking that he heard the faint sounds of a piano playing for about 30 seconds before the cassette clicked dead.

CHAPTER 30

James rose abruptly from the chair, still replaying what Kelly had told Dr. Brookside on the tape over and over in his mind. He placed the cassette player back into his bag. "How could she have disappeared into thin air? Did she leave the room without the doctor noticing? And... that shadowy figure, was it real, or was it my imagination playing tricks on me again?" James asked himself. He turned towards the office door. "Fuck! This isn't good," he exclaimed, coughing up a dark wet glob of blood into the palm of his hand.

James wiped the blood on his pants leg and walked toward the closet. He grabbed the round brass doorknob and tried to turn it. Nothing; it refused to budge. He jiggled the knob several times. "This one's locked, too. Damn, this is just great. I don't have time for this shit. It's time to get out of this place!" James told himself. He looked back at the room one last time before heading through the main door, finding himself once again in the grimy halls.

"Okay, now, all I have to do is find the last page. I can go home and see my family again." James dug through the burlap sack and took out the map. He checked the map to look for the next spot and see how far away it was. As he pored over the chart James noticed a mark he had never seen on the map before. A bright circle was now marked in orange ink. "Wait, that wasn't here before? How did it appear?" He saw the word 'basement' written a few inches above the new mark. "So, that mark also looks to be on the first floor as well. I guess I need to head there next, then," James said as he put the map back in his bag and started making his way to the stairs once more.

As he continued to walk the halls James could hear what sounded like faint tapping on some of the covered windows. Is that rain? He thought. The door for the stairway was located just a few feet away. "I need to find the last torn page. Once I have it, I can get out of this place and reunite with my family."

James opened the door to the stairway, slowly starting his descent downward. As he was getting closer to the first floor he couldn't help but wonder why someone hid a hand-drawn map in this place. "Did the same thing happen to them?" he asked himself as his eyes stared off into space, hand draped across his chin in a thinker pose. The lack of food and lost blood wreaking immense havoc upon his body. His overall strength and his eyesight were fading. James could feel his body painfully breaking down from the inside. It was now cannibalizing itself for nutrition. He had some momentary doubts if he would ever see his wife or child again. He wondered if his fate lay in death within this hospital. The people who were here before him were all victims of Dr. Coffin's cruel experiments. James still had no idea who brought him to this place and why. The only lead he could go on with was the fact that he had tried to defend this person in a court case years ago.

The only sound echoing throughout the stairway was the click-clank sound of James' cane hitting the steps as he walked downward. He finally reached the bottom, exhausted. Twenty long minutes flowed by before he reached the first floor. James opened the door to the main hallway, observing the corridor. He noticed a door that he hadn't seen before in the distance. "Hmm, I guess maybe that's where I need to go?" James muttered, stepping foot onto the gritty, icy title ground of the first floor.

He felt an overwhelming presence pulling him towards the unexplored doorway. "I wonder what, exactly, is it?" James remarked as he walked towards it. The black door was a solid, ten-inch-thick piece of wood made from oak, appearing to have a charcoal texture. "Was this door always here? I don't remember seeing it last time I was here." He said. "Maybe I just never noticed it. I was so focused on other stuff every time I came down here."

James could not shake the feeling that this door was new. "Well, I have to find that last page. I need to punch the code into the front door, scan the badges, and go home. What is in this room?" he asked himself. James grabbed the doorknob and tried to turn it. "Damn. My luck, huh? It's locked." James was disappointed. He took a few steps back away from the door to inspect it. Letting out a small sigh, he turned and proceeded further down the hallway.

James paused for a brief moment to examine the map again. He was trying to find out how to get down to the basement. James noticed that the map showed only three rooms, but here he could clearly see a fourth door before him. *Wait a second, the map earlier showed the fourth door on this floor. It was even circled in orange, the word 'basement' written on top of it. But now the map shows that the first floor has three doors again? I'm losing my mind; I need to get out of here. Just what the hell is up with this door?* he considered.

"This door has to lead to the basement," James told himself as he continued looking at the map. "How the hell am I going to get down there if the damn thing is locked?"

A loud creaking sound echoed throughout the hallway, coming from the ashen door. James turned around; it was now unlocked and wide open. James stood puzzled, looking at the opening.

“It was… it was locked shut. I couldn’t even budge it… how did it…? Who opened the door?” he said, wondering once again what the hell had been going on. As James walked closer to the open doorway, he could hear the faint whispers of people talking in the dark chamber. He couldn’t make out what they were saying, their words sounding foreign. All James knew was that it had to be a group of between eight and twelve people, nothing to laugh at. “I wonder what they’re talking about?” James asked himself, grabbing his flashlight out of the burlap sack.

He turned it on and slowly walked into the room. It laid before him empty; No desk, chairs, file cabinets, or even rats or insects scurrying across the walls. The only thing in the room, in the center, was a set of rickety, wooden steps leading down into a seemingly endless void. With immense caution James his way down the steps, hoping that they wouldn’t break under his weight. James shined the bright beam of light into the dark abyss.

The stairs creaked and cracked with every step he took. There were rotten holes scattered throughout the platforms, ancient age clearly showing in the dim flashlight. They felt as if they were in danger of breaking at any moment. The further down James went into the darkness, the louder the voices of the group was growing. He approached the bottom of the steps and another door appeared before him. It appeared the same as the door at the top of the stairwell, blackened in ashes as if a fire had once damaged its’ surface. A small yellow light was fixed above the doorway, flickering. The air felt heavy with dreadful anticipation as James panned the flashlight along the stairway walls. James barely noticed that the passageway had narrowed as he descended the steps until he suddenly found it was incredibly difficult to move around.

He took the map out of his bag, looking to see if there was a layout for the basement, but the only reference the map contained was the orange circular marking. He grabbed for the handle to open the door, only to realize that it didn't feature one of any kind upon its' surface; it didn't even have a hole from where a handle could have previously fallen off. "How the fuck am I supposed to open this door with no God damn doorknob!" James bellowed in anger. He looked at the door a bit closer and could see that there were four iron bolt locks. "These are the same bolt locks that you would find on the doors in public restrooms. Maybe if I just..." James said as he reached for one of the mechanisms to unlock the bolts. "Yes! I've got it!" he said. "Easy enough." He twisted the other three-bolt locks. After he removed each of them, James pushed on the door to see if it would budge.

The thick wood fell slowly to the floor, in a chillingly unnatural way. A thick cloud of dust kicked up from the ground as the boom of the crashed wooden door echoed throughout the building. A bright light blinded James for a moment. He opened his eyes, black spots dancing within his sight as he rubbed them with his hands, trying to refocus his vision.

James could still hear chatter coming from the group of people in the basement. *Who are they? Is my mind once again playing tricks on me?* James wondered, still clearing the spots from his eyes. He leaned onto the wall for support as he made his way into the room. James used his cane as a blind person would to help himself keep balance. He stretched his cane out a couple of feet in front of himself and tapped it on the ground. He swept the tip from left to right, while maintaining his leaning position on the left-hand wall.

"This fucking sucks," he told himself as he made his way into the darkened room. The talking was getting louder now.

His sight began to return and James could begin to see the outlines of people emerge. He still couldn't make out much detail about them yet but he knew that there were a lot more people present in the area than he had first thought. A bright flash engulfed the room.

CHAPTER 31

"James? James? Hey man, are you okay?" A man was standing next to him. James once again rubbed his eyes and his sight began to return to him.

"Where am I?" James asked in a daze. The voice was laughing at him. "You're at your wedding, man, how could you forget? You must have had a lot more to drink last night than we thought," it replied.

The voice was strong and deep. James looked at the guy. "Jake?" he said, confused.

"Man, you are one lucky son of a bitch marrying Liz," Jake said with an enthusiastic smile, nudging James' right arm.

"This can't be real, my wedding was many years ago," James whispered, still taken aback a bit, trying to piece together what was going on. "No, this can't be right. I was standing in a small hallway. I opened the door... and then, the next thing I remember was a bright flash of light. So how the hell am I here? No, this isn't right, this has to be some another dream or hallucination. I should be back inside the hallway of the abandoned hospital."

"Hospital?" Jake replied. "What hospital? James, are you okay? You're not getting cold feet, are you.?"

"No," replied James, looking at Jake. "I just... I don't know."

"Okay, I'm just checking," Jake said with a worried look on his face.

James looked across the room, spotting a sea of people sitting down. Sitting at the front were close friends and family of the bride and groom; behind them were scores of acquaintances and coworkers of Liz and James. He soon realized he was in a church, the same church where he and Liz were married. The bright sunlight shining through the multicolored stain glass windows had brightened up the church in a warm glow. Each guest was dressed in their Sunday best. Men wore suits of different styles, mostly black but some had on dark blue. James even spotted someone wearing a tan suit in the crowd, and another man with one appearing light gray. All the women sported lovely dresses, colors ranging all over the spectrum of the rainbow. The pews were filled to the brim.

James then looked toward Jake, who was standing right next to him. *He must be my best man, I mean, must have been my best man. But why can't I remember what happened on that day? Why?* James thought, on edge. He looked at the other three men. They were all wearing identical four-button, black double-breasted suits. James then turned and looked at the bridesmaids. Each one had on a lovely, light blue sleeveless dress that puffed out towards the bottom.

James still tried to wrap his head around what was taking place. The pianists began to play. As the music filled the room, one by one all everyone in the building began to stand up. The crowd turned towards the grand church doors and watched with eager anticipation. They were awaiting the arrival of James' beautiful bride. Even James now found himself staring toward the cathedral entrance, deeply anticipating Liz's appearance.

"Not getting cold feet, huh, buddy?" Jake asked with a smile.

"No, I'm just… um…"

"Just what?" Jake asked, worry starting to overtake his voice.

"I'm simply happy, that's all. This is… overwhelming," James said with a sense of unease. He did not want to tell Jake that he thought this was another trick of his mind, or that he believed this was all a dream.

"That's good, man. I am so happy for you." Jake patted his friend on the shoulder. They, along with everyone else in the building, watched as people streamed down the aisle. A little girl, about nine years old, who looked a little bit like Amber spread small pink and red flower petals on the ground.

After moments had passed slowly, there standing directly across from James was Liz. She was the most beautiful woman in the entire church. The elegant white lace wedding dress she wore hugged her body and magnified her features. The transparent mesh veil covering her face held a certain mystique about it. The sleeves featuring patterns of white rose across them brought a kind of magnificence to her dress. A long train finished toward the bottom of the dress. It appeared almost as if a mermaid's tail was dragging along the ground as she walked.

James' eyes were fixated on Liz. All the worries and fears that anything bad was going to happen seemed to just disappear the closer she got to him. *Huh, I don't remember Liz wearing a veil, but it's been such a long time… maybe she might have.* James thought to himself. He watched as his soon-to-be lovely wife walked down the aisle towards him. His heart was beating faster now as she came close, feeling as if it were about to pound heavily forth from his chest. The glow of the sun's light resonated from her dress. In front of Liz were two small kids. One was a boy dressed in a black suit, carrying a white pillow with two rings on the top. One was gold, the other one silver, with a clear gem on top.

The other was a girl in a beautiful white dress holding a basket of rose pedals. *Another flower girl?* James wondered, curious. *Strange. She also reminds me of Amber when she was that age.*

Everyone watched with smiles on their faces as Liz made her way to the altar. James smiled. "I'm so happy," he whispered to Liz as he took her hands, wanting so badly to lift the veil so that the pair could kiss.

"Me, too," Liz replied. They both turned toward the priest as everyone else in the building took their seats. James and Liz stood side-by-side in front of the priest and began to speak. The man recited every word from the rites of marriage as well as several select quotes from the Bible. James could not help feeling something was wrong, very wrong. The priest looked at Liz and began to speak once more.

"Do you, Elizabeth Mary Albright, take this man, James Michael Callaway, to be your lawfully wedded husband before the grace of God, to love and to cherish, for richer, for poorer, in sickness and in health, to love and to cherish until death do you part?"

"I do" Liz replied, a single tear emerging down her cheek as she looked into James' eyes.

"Do you, James Michael Callaway, take this woman, Elizabeth Mary Albright, to be your lawfully wedded wife before the grace of God, to love and to cherish, for richer, for poorer, in sickness and in health, to love and to cherish until death do you part?"

James looked at Liz. It seemed as if a lifetime had passed before he spoke. "I... I... I... don't," James said, looking directly into Liz's eyes.

"I'm... I'm sorry? Can you repeat that? I thought you said... no?" the priest asked James. The groom turned and looked at the priest. "I will not marry her," he told the collared man, firmness in his tone.

Light chatter began to grow into an uproar from the crowd of people watching. Liz backed up a few steps. "James!" she cried out, sadness evident in her voice as tears ran slowly down her face. "Don't you love me anymore?"

"I do, I love my wife very much," he replied.

"Then, why won't you Marry me?" Liz asked.

"Because..." said as he looked down toward his left hand, at an indent where a wedding ring was once located. He began to rub the fourth finger on his left hand with his right index finger in a circular motion, staring at the mark in a trance-like state.

"Because what do you mean, James, because what?" Liz said, shaken by the answer.

"Because..." he said to her, still massaging the mark on his finger, "you are not my wife!" James shouted in immense anger as he looked up at her. His eyes showed a fiery hatred within them. The loud chatter that rang throughout the church suddenly stopped. The bright warm light of the sun instantly turned cold as the sun itself turned darkish red, almost the color of blood. The skies that once were shining through the windows as a beautiful blue was now a rusty, reddish black. James started to look around. The church shook violently as the walls burst into flames.

The firestorm quickly burned away at the dried, aged wood of the church. A loud siren pierced the sky as some of the guests were starting to transform. They were no longer human in appearance; they were morphing into abominable creatures that each possessed no discernable face. These monsters' limbs grew long and lanky, their nails growing uncontrollably into fine, pearly white sabers. Other guests simply burst into thick clouds of ashen dust.

Liz grabbed James by his shoulders. "You will be ours!" she said in a deep, unnatural voice.

"Liz!" James screamed, his voice shaken. The creature pretending to be his wife began to transform, her fingers turning into bird-like talons, the digits nearly a foot long and razor-sharp. James pushed her away.

"I knew you weren't my wife!" he shouted as he backed up. She laughed. "You're right; I'm not Liz. You are never going to see Liz again," it said as the once lovely, white, laced wedding dress turned into a moldy, gray-stained hospital gown. The garment was tattered, adorned with countless tiny holes. The entity ripped off its' veil, revealing not long, autumn hair but scraggly, white, mossy tendrils that fell directly onto the floor. The creature possessed a bald, cracked head adorned only with a handful of white whiskers atop its' dome. The scalp was blackened; it was a very deep, burnt charcoal, the kind you would find on a severe burn victim.

The creature's solid black, soulless eyes were locked onto James. It spoke now with a voice as deep and abysmal as the dark pits of eternity. "I am the one called Xol'hasan, and you will remain my possession forever." The demon now stood beyond ten feet tall and looked to still be growing. James looked around at the calamity surrounding him. The church was no more; in its' place now was a nightmarish hellscape. People were screaming in pain as they were being tortured. Some were set on fire repeatedly, their flesh bubbling and melting from their bones and then promptly growing back. Others had the skin peeled straight from their muscles, the layers regenerating mere moments later only for the baking sheets to slide once more from their flesh like melted butter. The young girl from the wedding party, along with the group of men involved in the ensuing orgy, began transforming into large, horrific, gelatinous creatures. The bodies were large, pink and slimy, like that of an overgrown hog that had just been skinned. Puss-filled organs hung from their extremities, exhibiting forth a foul, skunky stench as yellowish-green slime splattered everywhere. Despite all this, these abominations continued to fuck cheerfully upon the ground.

"You can't escape James. This is where you belong." Xol'hasan said, a piercing, otherworldly laugh filling the air.

"No! This can't be! I need to get out of this hospital. I need to see my family!" James cried to himself as he watched on. Xol'hasan then positioned himself mere inches from James' face. "You'll see them soon enough," he told James with a sickening smile, revealing what appeared to be dozens of rows of sharpened human canines. The teeth were covered in a thick, yellowish film. Maggots were wriggling in and out of small cavities present throughout the creature's mouth. James looked up at Xol'hasan and pushed him hard in the chest. "No, you're wrong!" yelled James in anger. "I will get out of this place and I will see my wife and daughter again. You and this God-forsaken fucking place can go back to the Hell you came from."

James then dashed down the aisle, dodging every unholy creature and tortured soul as he did. As he ran, he surveyed the field of bodies before him. One was that of a young man in his late twenties. His flesh was being ripped from him like aged duct tape by several child-like imps. "Help me!" the guy cried with tears running down his face as he looked at James. The demon-spawn children looked at James with orange, glowing eyes as they ripped handfuls of the man's flesh and shoved it in their mouths. Blood gushed out from their lower lips, running down malformed chins as they smiled at James. James froze for a moment as he remembered seeing these same children elsewhere in the hospital.

The second person James locked eyes with was an eighty-nine-year-old woman being repeatedly impaled by large iron rods. "Help me, please!" the old woman cried. James looked at her. "I'm sorry, I can't," he moaned as he headed for the door. The painful cries and demonic laughter grew into an ear-piercing roar as James made it to the exit. He pushed the door open and was instantly engulfed by a flash of light once again.

CHAPTER 32

James awoke in a small, damp, dark hallway. He sat up, his body facing the door. “What the fuck was THAT?” he said to himself. “Was that real? My imagination can’t be… THAT active, can it?” James took a deep breath as he stood up. He reached to open the door but abruptly stopped. “I could have sworn I pushed this door off its’ hinges,” James said, looking at the charred, blackened wooden plank was still fixed to its’ frame. James pushed his thoughts to the back of his mind, trying to dismiss the fever dream, or whatever that experience had been. He grabbed the handle to the door and, this time, there was no bright flash when it swung neatly open, ignoring the thought that the door hadn’t had any sort of knob adorning its’ surface before he blacked out. Heavy layers of dust fell from the top of the entranceway. James shined his flashlight into the dark chamber before him. To his surprise, the door didn’t lead to a room, but a long network of underground catacomb tunnels.

When James pointed the light down the passageway, he could see multiple tunnels branching out from the main corridor. His flashlight beam reflected off of the dark red bricks. James could see small droplets of condensations hugging the stone walls, the damp moisture glistening as it reflected it the light. He began walking down the gloomy, narrow tunnel. As he strode further into the catacombs James could once again hear the twitching of rats as they ran along the stone floor. “Where the hell am I going?” James asked himself as he glanced down each branching tunnel. One of the passages on the right led to a small area closed up by a chain-link cage; behind this fence laid two large electrical panels.

"Well, so I don't get lost, I guess I'll keep going straight." As James continued down the hallway he couldn't shake off the images of what he had seen, or at least, what he thought he had seen. He wondered if he could have helped those people. To even think about helping them would have been acknowledging that the entire experience was, in fact, real. James never believed in ghosts, the paranormal, or even the afterlife. His job concerned nothing but facts. Even now, though, he was thinking, What if...? He could probably explain everything that had transpired due to the lack of nutrition or blood loss, but he wasn't so sure of this as he had been earlier.

The light beam to fade even more. "Shit, I hope the light doesn't die on me down here," James said as he tapped the butt of the flashlight several times with the palm of his hand. "Man, this tunnel seems to go on forever. Please, God, let this flashlight hold up." He stopped and turned around briefly to look behind him for just a moment. A cold gust of wind ran up the back of his neck. James shivered briefly before looking in front of him. "Where the fuck am I going?" he said again, confused and frustrated now. He dug into the burlap sack to pull out his map and take a look at it, but it was of no use to him. It only had the word basement written on it. There were no drawings of the catacombs made available to him.

He began to ponder memories of Amber and Liz and the happy times the three of them shared. A smile came over James' face when he reminisced on his daughter's sixth birthday party. How she ran up to him when she lost a tooth. The fun games they would play together when she was four. How Liz spent all night baking a pink princess castle cake for Amber's third birthday. How his daughter's face lit up when she opened up her gifts. He thought wistfully of him and his brother-in-law Jeff playfully shoved half of Amber's birthday cake into his wife's face.

He even reminisced about his little girl running into their bedroom at night to sleep in between Liz and James when she had a bad dream. How Liz would make his favorite meals whenever he asked. The nights Liz and James would watch TV and cuddle on the sofa. She would tell him about her dreams of owning her baking shop and calling it Baby Cakes.

The air was now becoming dry and heavy as James kept thinking of Liz and Amber. He moved forward down the tunnel. His pain in his leg was becoming more and more unbearable by the second. James knew he had to get the front door operational so that he could finally leave and see his family. As James continued walking the dark hallway, he heard the sound of a door creep slowly open behind him. The noise made by the rusted hinges of the door made his heart raced several beats faster. James was frozen in fear for a moment. He slowly turned to look behind him. He could see a large metal door fully opened and what looked to be a flickering blue light coming from the room.

"Where the hell did that room come from?" James asked. He cautiously walked towards this newly opened door. Once he reached to opening, James peeked inside. The chamber was almost completely dark except for a small blue bulb in the center of the ceiling. The light was flickering at a crazed pace. The fixture emitted a humming noise as if to signal that the light could be snuffed out at any minute. James walked into the room; all that located inside was an old white projector screen, rolled down. Along the back wall was the corresponding projector seated upon a small metal table. James swept the flashlight across the room, looking around to see if there was anything else in here. The room was just like the hallway: aged reddish brick walls that were cold and damp to the touch.

Why would someone have a projector room down here? James wondered as he walked towards the ancient machine. It sat in the middle of the small table. The table was constructed from thin metal, with spots of rust covering its' legs as well as its' surface area. Everything in the room was caked in a thick layer of dust. James wiped the powder from the lens of the projector. "I don't know why I'm doing this. This thing looks to be a piece of shit; it's probably too old to even turn on anymore, let alone project images properly."

James remembered that he had picked up a film reel and placed it in his burlap sack. He dug into the bottom of the bag and pulled out the old tape reel. It felt like he had found this in a room a lifetime ago now, given everything he's been through in this horrid place. James set up the project and, after some fiddling, managed to get the reel setup inside the aged device. James took a breath and pressed Play. The projector heated up and rumbled a bit before it turned on. James walked backward for a bit as the projector hummed loudly.

The projector flickered several times before the film began to play. A black and white image of Dr. Coffin graced the film screen. He was sitting on the edge of his desk, discussing to the camera what he was going to do to one of the patients and how it will help his studies. The film quickly jumped to a scene with a few nurses down in the basement. The area was dimly lit, flickering lights burning from a few lit candles that were fastened inside iron holders affixed to the brick wall. The glow shined just bright enough to make out the image of a male patient. James could see that the young man was heavily sedated and strapped to an old gurney. The bed was placed in the middle of a large stone archway deep inside these very catacombs. In the video, James could see what looked to be a small platform of some kind. On this table was the skull of an animal James could not identify and a large drawing of a five-star upside-down pentagram. Next to the skull were a small, leather-bound book and a bronzed knife.

The tome was open and rested on a metal book stand. James could see something written in the volume but couldn't make it what it said out due to the graininess of the film.

A roach scurried across the screen as the video showed Dr. Coffin and the nurses wearing pitch-black robes. The nurses formed a circle around the man and began to chant rough syllables in a language sounding like none James had ever heard throughout his life. "A'hu ti'shui lu'zu, a'hu ti'shui lu'zu, haz'tu di'fjiuha ishe ha'ibs c'aito." The patient on the gurney was completely naked except for a pair of white boxer shorts. He appeared paralyzed yet wide awake while they kept repeating the chant, over and over. James could see the fear plainly in the man's eyes as tears raced down his cheeks.

Dr. Coffin picked up the bronzed knife from the ritual stand. It featured strange markings carved into its' bone-clad handle and runic symbols etched completely down the blade. James couldn't make out any of the shapes of the symbols upon the blade. The film jumped over to another scene, fuzz covering the scene as it did. Now, it showed Dr. Coffin and the nurses hovering closely over the man. The nurses continued their chant as Dr. Coffin placed the sharp edge of the blade on the man's neck. "A'hu ti'shui lu'zu, a'hu ti'shui lu'zu, haz'tu di'fjiuha ishe ha'ibs c'aito." The cold steel of the knife pierced the skin of the man's throat, splitting his neck muscles apart as the blade dug deeper, cutting the man's throat wide open. Blood poured out of his neck like running water. James continued to watch in horror as he knew that the person on that gurney felt every inch of the blade dig into his flesh but couldn't move. The nurses quickly gathered the blood into a slivered goblet. After the goblet was filled, each of the nurses stood near one of the four limbs of the now-deceased patient. Dr. Coffin walked over and stood just a foot in front of the head.

A nurse handed the blood-filled goblet to the doctor. He raised this goblet over the head of the dead man and spoke more words from the strange, forgotten language. He then pressed the rim of the goblet to his lips and drank, passing it to the nurse on his left. Each nurse took a drink from the bowl and then passed it to the next nurse down until the goblet made its' way around the circle and back to Dr. Coffin. Moments later James could see that they now sported a crimson stain upon their faces, covering their lips down to their necks.

A chill ran down the back of James' neck as the video showed Dr. Coffin slowly walking to the camera. The candle to his right flickered wildly as he shook his head, declaring that the ritual was a failure. He wiped the blood from his glasses with the left sleeve of his black robe. *"We should have better luck with the next one,"* he told the camera as he closed a tiny black book he had been holding in his right hand. The film then fades to white; after a few seconds, the projector stops.

"What the hell did I just watch?" James asked himself as he walked over to the projector. He looked the machine over as he wondered what happened to the rest of the film that wasn't shown, and why it was cut short. More questions plagued his mind as he searched the room. "There is nothing else in here. I feel like I just wasted my time," he mumbled in frustration as he stared at the blank screen. Something in the upper left corner caught his eye; it was a number lightly carved into the projector. James got a bit closer to try and make out what was written. The number was *0*. James wondered if this was the last number he needed to get the gate opened.

He placed the flashlight in his mouth and took out one of the papers, along with a pen, writing the number on it. James then made his way out of the room. With no time to waste, he rushed for the door to the basement stairwell to bring himself back onto the first floor.

As he ran through the dark catacombs he once again heard laughing emanating all around him. James didn't stop this time as he blocked out the laughter as well as the pain in his leg; his only goal now was to get to the door.

James could see the door and the wooden steps. "Yes, I am close! Liz, Amber, Daddy is coming home!" He shouted. James stopped; the hallway was now quiet. "What happened to the laughter?" James asked himself, puzzled and feeling a bit nervous as he turned around to look down the dark tunnel. His flashlight only reached so far down the tunnel, barely lighting it up.

James could hear a faint noise coming from deep within the black abyss. It was the sound of rusted metal scraping against stone. James stared into the darkness as the racket inched closer with incredible speed. A tall, thin, twisted demon emerged into the light as it continued to make its' way towards James. In its hand was the bronzed knife James had seen on the projector film. Its' black fingers were wrapped tightly around the hilt. The demon's head was twisted one hundred and eighty degrees, facing towards' its' backside. James' eyes filled with fear as he uttered the name *Xol'hasan* in a growling hiss. The creature's head twisted around to the front of its' body, dark red eyes pierced through the dim light. A smile flooded upon its' face, taking over every visible feature.

James turned around and quickly ran up the wooden steps. He found his way to the metal door blocking the exit to the building. He held the flashlight between his teeth as he searched the burlap sack for the three ID cards, quickly taking them all out. James felt as if his heart were going to burst from in his chest as he placed a badge inside each of the three card slots. To his surprise, nothing happened. There was no beep or telltale sign. The number pad didn't light up.

He took the key cards out and reinserted them back into the slots in a different pattern to see if this would do anything, but still nothing. "Fuck! It was supposed to light up after all three ID badges were put in," James yelled out, frustrated.

He looked around the room. "Wait," he said to himself, thinking. "This building has not been operating in who knows how many years. Maybe the door is operating on main power," James said as he recalled seeing the two electrical panels down in the basement. "One of those fucking switches has to turn the power back on to this God damn place." James placed all three ID cards inside the burlap bag, grabbed the flashlight with his hand, and proceeded to make his way back down to the basement.

Making his way down the wooden stairs, James was more nervous now then he had ever been. He had almost tasted freedom. The flashlight once again barely illuminated the tunnel, but it was still enough for James to see. As James inched closer to the electrical panels in the basement, he swore that he could hear a voice emerging from deep within the darkness. *What is the voice trying to say?* James wondered. All he heard was what sounded like a mumble. James didn't attempt to respond to the voice; instead, he kept on walking as fast as he could down the tunnel towards the cage. After several minutes of trying to figure out what the voice was saying, James finally made an effort to stop listening. The voice now didn't seem to be talking, but rather, it was singing a song. It was one that James knew all too well: the lullaby his wife used to sing to put their daughter to bed when she was an infant.

A tear escaped James' eye as the song began to echo loud but softly throughout the dark tunnel. He closed his eyes for a moment as he began to have a flashback of his wife Liz sitting in a handmade wooden rocking chair, cooing Amber to sleep in her nursery.

His daughter's room had bright pink walls and drawings of animals, along with toys scattered on the bright cream carpet. James could still very clearly see his wife in the corner of the nursery humming the song as their little girl nestled her small head on Liz's chest to fall asleep. He opened his eyes, wiping tears away, determined not to be sucked into the full-blown flashback and whatever chaos awaited within. He pressed onward until he came upon the chain-linked cage housing the main electrical panels. The smell of fresh air overcame his senses. The memory of his wife's bad attempt at baking redfish flooded his vision. He could hear his daughter Amber begging for cash to spend at the school Fair. None of this mattered, he told himself. He was so close to escaping this old abandoned mental hospital. He had to retain his focus now.

CHAPTER 33

As he moved closer to the cage, James could hear thousands of roaches and rats scurrying along the walls and floors. James had a weird urge to peek into the room beside him, the same room that held the old projector. As he leaned in a bit, he shined the flashlight into the room. The machine was missing. "Huh? What This was the room, I know it was," he said, utterly baffled. The metal table, however, was still there, but a dark red, velvet cloth was draped over it. A silver goblet sat upon the center.

Shocked, James leaned over to inspect the goblet. It was no taller than a standard large drinking cup. There were marking carved all around the silver bowl. James shined the light inside the goblet. It was filled with a deep red liquid. Backing away, he then noticed that there was an upside-down animal skull and leather-bound book set just behind the bowl. "Oh, fuck... oh, fuck... this is the same setup that I saw in the film," James said, horrified.

A feeling of dread washed over him as he backed his way towards the door. He never took his eyes off the metal table as he did. Candles along the wall, previously unseen, had suddenly lit themselves. James panicked now, turned around and bolted out of the room. Despite the condition of his leg, he no longer felt the pain as pure adrenaline-fueled his escape.

James managed to make it to the chain-link gate. The metal forming it was aged and rusted. The gate wasn't locked, so James opened the cage door and walked right into the small, enclosed area. Two electrical panels and a small transformer James hadn't noticed before awaited his arrival.

He noticed that the first-panel door was swung wide open, and each breaker was switched to the "On" position, including the large, main breaker located at the top of the panel face. A sudden shiver rushed over him once more as icy wind slid past his arm. "Fuck it. I need to get out of this basement. I better hurry, I don't know how much longer I can be here." He opened the door on the second panel, and just like the first one, all the breakers were set to "On." All except for one, this panel's main breaker. He flipped the switch and, second later, he could hear a low humming sound emit from the transformer. "I hope that does he!" he said, jogging out of the cage. A second icy gust flowed past him, sending shivers up his spine.

James shook his head as he could hear his name being called from deep within the abyss of the catacombs. He ran as fast as he could for the basement door. As he stepped onto the wooden stairway, a deep rugged voice asked from within the darkness, "How's your head, James?" He froze in terror.

"Who… who's there?" he asked, stuttering.

"Why, James, I am your friend," the voice replied. "I am the one who's been helping you escape from this place."

"You… what? Helped me?" Now James was confused. He could sense the man – or, thing – moving rapidly towards him now. Whatever it was, it didn't make a sound as it glided along the floor. "Yessss," the voice hissed back in reply.

Long, boney fingers pierced out from the darkness, stretching out towards James' neck. "Come on, James, let me help you get out of this dreadful place. I know Liz and Amber must be worried sick about you." James' heart raced, but he remained silent.

"Don't you trust me, James?" the thing asked as its' fingers were now inches away from James.

"No!" he shouted back, and James up the stairs. He looked behind him to see thick, black smoke racing towards him. As he got to the top of the stairwell, he opened the door to the first floor and was greeted by a smoke-filled corridor. An unseen force pushed him down onto the floor.

When the smoke cleared, James found himself lying face down in the cell he'd awoken inside several times before. "What the hell? What am I doing back here?" he asked as he picked himself back off the ground. As James walked out into the hallway, a loud static sound came over the speaker as the P.A. system sprang to life.

"Having fun yet, James?" the voice asked, the same voice that assaulted him in the basement. "Ever since you came here, you have been breathing an odorless gas that has been pumping silently through the vents of this hospital. Its' effects include hallucinations and delusions, among other things. Oh, by the way... the injection you gave yourself earlier, well, let's just say that it was a trial run drug code-name T18B1." James stood in disbelief at what he was being told. "Better run, James, you're no fun to us if you don't run." A long, drawn-out laugh was emitted before the speakers cut out once more.

James snapped out of his trance just in time to see long shadowy arms begin to protrude from the walls. They began reaching out towards James, trying to grab him. As James tried to run down the hall he soon noticed even more arms and hands appearing from the walls. They were now coming out of the ceiling. Not caring anymore, armed with the knowledge that they were, indeed, hallucinations, James burst through the door to the stairwell.

A jolt of adrenaline-filled him as jogged down the stairs feeling like an Olympic track star, feeling zero pain as he did so. He didn't bother stopping for any reason James until he made it back to the first floor. He bolted out of the stairway and ran to the main door. The dark shadow hands were still coming out of the walls, but James paid them no mind. He once again grabbed the three ID cards from his bag and put them in the slots. James kept looked behind him while he was doing this. He then saw all the lights turning off one by one as a smoke cloud was coming down the hall. *Fuck, I have to hurry!* James said as all three ID cards where placed in their slots. *Now, the moment of truth.* He flipped the switch on the door.

The smoke cloud was getting closer to James by the second. He could hear what sounded like screams of pain emanating from deep within the cloud. "No, I will not die in this place. I will see my family again, I will hold my wife and daughter one more fucking time. Come on, you stupid fucking door!" he shouted as the keypad lit up. A bright smile came across his face. He then dug into his bag, pulling out all the torn pages. "Okay, now time for the eight digital code," James said, inputting multiple different combinations based on the eight numbers he found. The keypad kept displaying errors as none of the combinations worked. He was getting more and more frustrated as the darkness was now mere inches away from him. "Fuck!" he yelled. "Calm down, James." He took a few deep breaths and then input the code *87625037*. The light turned green and the door unlocked, much to James' surprise. "Yes!" he shouted he opened the door and made his way outside. James ran as fast as he could down the small concrete steps. He looked back only once. As he did, he watched the metal door slamming shut as the smoke cloud was about to escape the building. "That was close," he gasped, fresh air filling his lungs.

As he breathed in the midnight air he gazed upward toward the sky. “Ahh, the warm glow of the full moon feels even better outside!” he said, proceeding to walk briskly down the gravel driveway, which was covered in a thin layer of snowflakes, leading away from the building. The gate that normally blocked the outside world’s access to the abandoned sanitarium laid halfway open. “Liz, Amber, Daddy is finally coming home.”

As the cold night wind brushed across his face, James stopped and turn around looking at the old abandon hospital one last time. “Good fucking bye, and good riddance,” he said, turning to walk out of the gate and towards freedom. “Okay, now, which way do I go?” He peered left and right down the road. James had no clue where he was. James decided he would head down the right path, seeing the faint glow of city lights. “I guess I’ll go this way.”

He was not prepared for the freezing night air; it was now starting to get to him. “I should have l-looked for f-fucking warmer clothes, thi-this is b-bullshit. I can no longer f-feel my hands.” He still wore the old dirty rags from the hospital which did absolutely nothing to keep him warm. To make it even worse, he was also barefoot. He was hoping that a car would pass by any moment and offer him a ride.

After what felt like an hour and a very grueling walk, an old blue Firebird slowly drove up to James. The car stopped and the passenger window slowly rolled down. Cautiously, James turned his head toward the car as the lights inside clicked on. James spotted a yellow New York license plate hanging from the front, between headlights. A middle-aged white male greeted him.

“Hiya fella,” the man said to James, heavily accented. "Ya don’t look good, pal.”

"No, I'm not. I've been to Hell and back tonight... literally," James replied.

"Say buddy, tell ya what. I'm goin' to tha city, why don'cha hop on in an' I'll bring ya to the hospital?" the driver said.

"No! Oh, no, no more hospitals for me now, just take me to the police station, please," James as he opened the door and climbed inside the car. "Straight to the Police station," he reiterated, clicking on his seatbelt.

"Whateva ya say, buddy. Police station it is," the driver said as the car took off.

"So... what in the hell happened to you, if ya don't mind me asking?" the driver asked James a minute into the ride. James didn't reply; he just stared out the car window, watching the trees rush past his window, catching glimpses of the moon in the forest. They drove down the long road with nothing but woods on each side. James took a deep breath. He didn't quite recognize this area off hand. He finally told the driver, "I'd rather not talk about it."

Both men remained quiet during the rest of the ride. All James could think about was his wife and daughter. "Okay, buddy, here we are... I wish you luck, pal," the driver said with a smile on his face as James exited the vehicle. "Thank you very much," he told the driver. "I'm sorry, I didn't even ask you your name."

"It's Adam," the driver replied.

James smiled. "Well, thank you Adam for the ride." He closed the passenger door and James watched as Adam drove off in the direction the pair had come.

James walked into the Police station, which was loud and busy with cops and criminals. The rush of noise was overwhelming to James as he walked up to the help desk. “Hello,” James said to a deputy sitting down at the front counter. As the man looked up, James noted the name plastered on his badge: K. Webster. He was a rather large man, no older than thirty-eight-years old, but his short, dark curly hair was already receding. His pudgy face was smooth and clean except for a drop of ketchup up that hung on his chin. Years of working the graveyard shift had done a toll on his body as large, dark bags hung under his eyes. “Hey, are you okay, sir?” the deputy asked James.

“I need some help. Who is in charge?” James asked the man.

“My God, what the hell happened to you? We need to call the paramedics for you, sir. You need to go to the hospital immediately. You are covered in deep wounds and your clothes are all stained in blood,” the deputy replied.

“No!” James shouted at him. “I need to speak with whoever is even in charge here.”

“That would be me,” a woman’s voice said from behind James. He turned around.

“Hi, are you in charge of this station?” James asked the woman.

“Yes. I am Lieutenant Elizabeth Breyer. I am in charge here. What is your name, sir?”

“My name is James Callaway.”

“Okay, James. Now, why would you come all the way here without going to the hospital first?” Lt. Liz asked James.

"Can we go somewhere with less noise and talk in private?" James asked her.

"Yes, we can talk in my office." Lt. Liz replied, opening the door and leaving the way for James.

James and the Lieutenant made their way inside the office. She handed him a cup of water and a snack cake from the vending machine then sat in her chair. James happily downed the snack cake and drank the water. "Thank you so, so much," James told her as he wiped his mouth with a small white napkin.

"So, why did you come here first, James? You look like you need some medical attention," she asked him. James explained to the Lieutenant what had happened to him. He spent a few hours telling her about the entire ordeal, waking up in the abandoned hospital, and how he was tormented by somebody calling himself Xol'hasan. Lt. Liz was taken back quite a bit by this story. The pair got up and walked out of her office once he was finally finished.

"Okay, Mr. James, we will start investigating exactly who kidnapped you and locked you away in old St. Mary's. In the meantime, I have called for some paramedics to come by and check on you," She told him.

"Okay, that sounds great," James replied, relived but very exhausted. "Any chance I get a cigarette, please? I haven't smoked since before I met my wife, but... I feel like I need one tonight."

"I'm sorry, but I don't have any on me. There are two deputies outside who smoke, though. I think one of them might have a pack."

"Okay, thank you," James said, walking outside.

James walked up to the two deputies. One was short and lean, sporting a professionally cropped gray beard, the name J. Walton etched upon his badge. The other one was taller and built not unlike a professional wrestler named S. Johnson. "Hey, umm, excuse me, but can I get a cigarette from one of you guys, please?" James asked them. Both of the deputies looked at James. Seeing how rough a shape he was in, Deputy Walton pulled a red box from his left pocket and offered it to James. He opened the top of the box, took out one cigarette, put it in his mouth, and handed it back to the tall deputy.

"Thank you. And umm, can I- "

Before James could finish, Deputy Johnson took out his Bic and lit the edge of the cigarette for him. "Thank you so very much," James said before walking a few feet away, just out of Walton and Johnson's sights.

He waited outside for the paramedics to pull up. As he was smoking the cigarette, he thought about all that he had gone through. Before he could begin to collect himself, he felt a hard, blunt object hit the back of his head. James was knocked unconscious onto the ground.

He woke up a few hours later, struggling to move. Wherever he had ended up, it was pitch black. After feeling around the darkness, he soon realized that he was inside a very tight wooden box. James could hear two men talking outside as well as what sounded like the banging of a hammer.

"Okay, I think this last nail should do it," One of the men said as he drove the last nail into the lid of the wooden box. "Now let's see how long it takes for that girl to escape the hospital. What was her name again, Amber?" the other man said, chuckling.

James banged his fist on the wooden lid as hard as he could, screaming. “Help, help me, please! Someone help me!” But his cries for help fell on deaf ears.

After a while, James finally broke out of the wooden box. To his surprise, he was outside of his home standing on the porch. “What the hell was that? What that another hallucination? The last thing I remember was smoking a cigarette at the police station.” He was completely puzzled.

“Hello?” he yelled out as he entered his house.

“Oh, James, thank God you’re home!” a female voice said from upstairs of the house.

“Li… Liz, is that you?” James cried. His wife ran downstairs, tears in her eyes as James scooped her into his arms, clutching her into the biggest hug he could muster. They both shared a passionate kiss.

“Where have you been?” she asked. “We were so worried about you. After you failed to come to Perez’s, Amber and I came back home. We filled a missing person’s report. Then,” Liz said as tears started to flow down her face again, “Then we saw on the news that your car was involved in an awfully bad wreck. The front end was smashed into a tree. We thought that’s where you were!” Liz broke down crying.

James pulled Liz close into him and buried her face into his chest. “It’s okay, hun, I’m back now, okay?”

“Oh, okay, James, I’m just happy you’re finally home,” she whispered back, tightening her hug around her husband.

“So, where have you been?” she asked.

"It's an incredibly long story, hun. I'll tell you and Amber all about it after I take a shower and rest up," he replied.

"By the way, where is Amber?" he asked Liz. "Amber is sleeping over at a friends' house tonight. We have the whole house all to ourselves," she said to him with a seductive smile.

James smiled back and kissed Liz. "Let me go take a shower first. After that, we can have a little fun, okay?"

"Okay, sweetie," Liz replied. She looked downward. "James, your leg, what happened?"

"I don't know. It must have been damaged when my car wrecked into the tree," he said as he walked upstairs to their bedroom.

James went into the bathroom, turned on the hot water, and started taking off his clothes. The hot water felt so great against it his skin. This is so incredibly refreshing, I can't believe it, he thought. As he was finished his shower, he wondered why Liz didn't ask him why he was wearing hospital clothes. *Oh, well. Maybe she was just too happy to see me.*

He finished washing up and turned off the shower. Dripping wet, James grabbed a towel to dry himself off. He walked up to the bathroom mirror. "Man, I desperately need a shave," he told himself as he picked up his razor and some shaving cream. He lathered his face up and started to shave. A few minutes later, he was back to sporting his normal smooth looks.

James walked out of the bathroom and into his bedroom where he found his wife Liz waiting for him, naked.

She was laying on the bed, legs spread open, and slightly bent in an upright position. James got into bed and crawled on the bed next to his wife. Liz, in a seductive voice, told her husband with a smile, “I don’t want to make love tonight, I just want you to fuck me.”

“Okay,” James said, smiling back as he began to kiss his wife. James began to grope Liz’s large, firm 32C cup breasts. He nibbled up and down the side of her neck as Liz moaned in pleasure. “It’s been a while since we just fucked,” she whispered in his ear, running one hand through his hair while the other snaked along his back. James’ right hand went in between her legs, rubbing her clit, inducing her into an even louder moment of ecstasy.

She could feel her husband’s fingers rapidly moving inside her. James was about to go down on her when Liz pulled his face toward hers. “I need you inside me now!” she told him, panting heavily. James shoved the full force of his member inside his wife, driving her crazy, fucking her quickly, madly. Her yelling was becoming loud, the bed slamming against the wall with more force after each stroke he took. The banging of the headboard echoed through the house, causing holes to form in the wall.

“Oh, fuck, James!” Liz screamed, now propped on all four limbs, moaning like a bitch in heat. James had his hands wrapped around her hair; every time he rammed his member deep inside her, he would pull her hair back towards him. Their bodies were covered in sweat and the melody of skin slapping together floated through the air as if it were a sweet symphony. Liz then asked James if she could get on top of him, and they switched positions. She began riding him like a bull, her breasts bouncing in rhythm as James watched. He grabbed her by the hips and started to fuck her even harder. Liz's eyes rolled back into her head with pleasure.

Liz then started to caress her own body. Her hands were moving from her stomach to her breast and back downward sensuously. They were verging on the edge of the climax together. Liz looked into James' eyes as she was riding him faster, smiling and whispering, "James, I love you."

"Oh, sweetie, I love you, too," he heaved back, breathlessly in passion.

Liz's expression began to change as she started to peel away at her own skin. James, caught in sudden surprise, stopped thrusting as horror flooded his eyes. His wife was ripping off layer after layer of her skin, laughing uncontrollably. Soon James could see his wife's exposed muscles, tendons, and nervous tissue. Bloody chunks of flesh hung from her, tattered into ribbons. Globules of blood fell upon James' naked body.

"What in the fuck!" James cried as his wife scratched ever more skin away from her body. She did it in a motion that reminded James of a child frantically tearing at a present on Christmas morning. "Get off of me... fucking creature! You're not my wife!" James cried as he tried to shove her off of him.

"Don't you love me, baby? Don't you think my body is sexy?" Liz said, looking into James' eyes with a seductive grin, peeling the skin from her face. The shards of flesh dangled, glistening with the horrific color of blood.

Her insides were now exposed, internal organs dangling, bouncing rhythmically as she continued to hump James' member. She leaned downward, her skinless face next to James' ear. "Fuck me now, James!" she whispered, licking the side of his face with her bloody tongue.

James screamed in horror her torn skin began to fuse into his flesh. It was transforming into the same shirt and pants he had worn when he was stranded in the asylum. The room was now in flames, ashes raining down onto the couple's bed that was morphing by the second into the dingy cell floor James had originally woken upon.

The sinew creature wore an impossible grin upon its' gore-ridden face. "I told you, James, you can never escape me," it told him before collapsing into dust. James sat up, his eyes wide with terror as he frantically began to look around the cell. He rubbed his hands along the cold, damp stone that formed its' walls, hoping that this was a nightmare and that he had simply fallen asleep in his bed.

He then ran to the cell's metal door, a panicked look in his face. He peered down at his own body and realized he was wearing a white, stained t-shirt as well as pajama pants; a patient ID bracelet graced his left wrist.

"No... No... NO! Let me out of here! Someone, please, help me! Help me!" he cried out, banging on the locked door. The shrill sounds of his voice echoed throughout the empty hallways of the abandoned hospital.

EPILOGUE

On the fourth floor of Saint Mary's Hospital, in the small town of New Jefferson, a young nurse with short, brunette hair was refilling a patient's IV bag as sunlight peeked through the semi-opened blinds. "How is the patient looking today, Nurse Brecka?" the doctor asked as he walked into the tiny, quiet hospital room.

"He looks good, doctor. His vital signs are all normal." She opened the blinds up a little more, allowing more sunlight to enter the room.

"Good, very good. Did you give him his daily injection of synthetic barbiturate?" the doctor asked.

"Yes, I just did." the nurse replied.

As the doctor turned to pick up the patient's chart, the nurse called out after him. "Dr. Brookside!" she said.

"Yes?" replied the doctor as he turned towards the nurse, looking the clipboard over.

"I was just wondering... why do we have to keep giving this guy this drug cocktail? Why do we have to keep him in a comatose state like this?" she asked.

Dr. Philip Brookside looked at the nurse. "Megan, this man was brought here six years ago. He was found guilty by the court for the murder of his family. He openly confessed to the judge that he raped and beat his wife and daughter every night, for four years, before slaughtering them in the basement of his family's restaurant."

"Every night, without fail, without mercy, for four years. After he killed them, he then cooked up some of their body parts and ate them. The rest, he had frozen, keeping some for himself and secretly incorporating the rest into the meals served at Perez's, the now-closed family restaurant."

Megan covered her mouth in horror as she couldn't believe what she was hearing. She had just arrived at the hospital two months prior; the nursing school hadn't prepared her for anything like this.

"After the cops raided his home and business, he tried to run, but he wrapped his car around a large tree. It was so mangled that it was a miracle he wasn't dead. His right leg was crushed badly; a metal rod impaled the back of his head, piercing his skull but barely missing his brain by millimeters. Being a defense attorney by trade, he attempted to represent himself in court, denying the court-appointed attorney afforded to him by the State. The evidence was just so overwhelming that the trial was over in just a day. The judge sentenced him to life without parole in Taneka State Penitentiary. Soon after he arrived, he got into a fight with another inmate. The night guards found him unconscious on the floor of the showers. He was then transported here to this hospital for medical care."

"Okay," Nurse Brecka said, "But that was six years ago. Why is he still like this? Shouldn't he have already been transported back to prison?"

"Well, once he regained consciousness, he tried to pick fights with the doctors and nurses who were trying to help him. So, the hospital administration placed a midnight call to Justice O'Connor's office requesting an order for the patient to be put into an induced coma until he the day the patient passed away. It was a new, experimental treatment that had just been approved by the State; knowing who this man was and the crimes he committed, Justice O'Connor's office faxed over the order within minutes of the request. This man is the State's pilot case for their new program, you could say. That's why he has two IVs hooked into the top of his hands. Each line pumps a mixture that keeps him alive but in the comatose state. But, if you ask me..." he said, looking at the patient now, "I think he is being tortured by his subconscious for what he has done." Dr. Brookside turned to leave the room.

"How can you tell?" she asked as he stepped into the doorway.

"Tell what?" the doctor replied, stopping and looking at the nurse.

"How can you tell he is being tortured subconsciously?"

"Well, after several weeks of seeing him twitch, and with the rapid eye movement, we brought in neurologist. He ordered the patient to be hooked to an EEG machine and the results... well, you see what state he's in." Dr. Brookside sighed. "Occasionally, despite the effects of the drugs, I see him silently mouthing off a word. It's always the same, every time. After a while, I determined he was trying to say someone's name... 'Hasan'. I have no idea who he's trying to talk to, though. God only knows." He walked out of the room, but not before adding, "You should probably go take your lunch now, Megan. You're looking a little pale."

Nurse Brecka walked over to the foot of the patient's bed. She picked up his chart and looked at his name, then looked up at him. His eyelids were closed, but she could tell his eyes were moving rapidly beneath them, left to right as if he could see something that wasn't there. His heart rate briefly increased, then settled down. His body was strapped tightly onto the bed. The nurse looked back down at the patients' name, then spoke it out loud, musingly, as she walked out of the room.

A few minutes later, Dr. Brookside returned to the patient's bedside with a small vial tucked into his palm. As he hovered over the comatose man, a smile began to creep upon his face. "Oh, little rabbit," he said. "The experiment is just beginning. It's time for you to go to hell, James Michael Callaway." He dumped the contents of the vial into the patient's IV.

A preview of....

THE ROAD

Breaking news: Livingston Parish deputies have called off their search for seven missing students from LSU. Police have uncovered zero leads that could be used to determine their whereabouts. Several weeks ago, the group was headed to a weekend retreat at a Maurepas cabin owned by one of the student's family members, but the family called police after the group never arrived.

"Without a single solid lead, I have made the difficult decision to pull my team of deputies away from the search. I will, instead, order three of my investigators to continue searching for either the students or evidence that could lead to their whereabouts. The one thing we managed to uncover was an empty blue Nissan Pathfinder located in the woods off Highway 22, but we could not find clues as to how it got there, nor where the passengers have ended up. I ask that the public please keep a lookout for the missing students.

To the families involved, I am so sorry we haven't been able to find your kids yet. You may want to prepare for the worst."

ABOUT THE AUTHOR

Gary Rome came into the world on June 25, 1985. When he's not busy writing, he loves watching movies or playing video games alongside his daughter, Raven. He also enjoys the outdoors, exercises religiously, and is a practitioner of Nordic Paganism.

He is a native of Marrero, Louisiana, and works full-time as a personal fitness guru in nearby Harvey. During his off time, you can often find him haunting one of the local bookstores on the Westbank.

Personal correspondence with the author can be sent via e-mail to:
garyrome@mail.com

The author can also be reached through his Twitter account:
@GaryERome

CPSIA information can be obtained
at www.ICGtesting.com
Printed in the USA
BVHW081021290123
657373BV00021B/281

9 781649 996343